About The Author

Joan M Moules is the author of over thirty books both fiction and non-fiction.

She also writes short stories and articles, runs occasional day workshops and is passionate about her writing. In junior school her desk was next to a window which looked across to a railway line and she was always in trouble for gazing across to the trains and making up stories about where the people on them were going instead of concentrating on what the teacher was saying. Eventually she was moved to the other side of the room where she couldn't see them... Some of her other interests, not in any special order, include reading, walking by the seashore, theatre, music hall, Victorian and Edwardian jewellery, cats and being with her family and friends. She is a member of The Society of Women Writers' and Journalists, Society of Authors, The Crime Writers Association and The Deadly Dames.

ISBN 9781912582266

Williams & Whiting (Publishers)

15 Chestnut Grove, Hurstpierpoint,

West Sussex, BN6 9SS

DAISY

Joan M Moules

Williams & Whiting

Chapter 1

The station was dirty. Bits of paper blowing about, cigarette ends and tin cans thrown on the ground. It was also busy with people hurrying between platforms as if there was no tomorrow. Panic hit Clare as an unkempt looking individual careered into her, almost knocking her new handbag from her shoulder. At first she thought that was what he was after, the money in the bag, but he was gone within seconds and without an apology, and her bag was intact.

She stood still in the midst of that bustling railway station and tried to find the calmness Robert said she normally generated. Thank heaven she had left in plenty of time, for how would she ever locate the right platform and train if she carried on in this way. If she missed it Robert would assume she had changed her mind about starting a new life with him, and would be borne off to Torquay without her.

What would he do if that happened? Would he search the train, and not finding her, return to his wife and try again? She didn't think so. 'That's been over for long while, Clare,' he said when she asked him that question, 'in any case I'm as sure as I can be that there's someone else for her too. I've tried to tackle the divorce thing so many times now, but she won't listen. My guess is that he's married too and...'

'Clear the way now, clear the way,' and she moved aside quickly as a lumbering railway tractor full of baggage almost ran into her. Standing her case on the

1

ground she consulted her watch. Plenty of time, all she had to do was find the platform then she could buy a cup of coffee and settle herself before she met Robert.

Five minutes later she was ensconced in the corner of the cafeteria and the noise and bustle of the station was muted. Mentally she checked everything. She had given up the flat, told her aunt that she was going abroad for two years with a newly formed ballet company, settled milk and paper bills, and let it be known amongst her friends that she was going to Italy. Everything to do with her old life was gone. She glanced at the shiny gold ring on the third finger of her left hand. Everything was new, even the ring Robert had given her two days ago.

'I'm as sorry as you that we can't do it properly, Clare,' he'd said, 'but I'd be a bigamist if I did. Believe me my darling I mean every word when I say, 'With this ring I thee wed, with my body I thee worship…' Tears filled her eyes and she opened the pristine handbag and took out a handkerchief. This wouldn't do at all. The past was finished and the future just beginning – their future, hers and Roberts. Swallowing the last of the coffee she slung her bag over her shoulder, picked up her smart new suitcase and walked back into the main body of the station.

She had only five minutes now to wait in the queue that had formed by the platform entrance. When the gate was opened she filed through with the others, showed her ticket, and walked to the third coach as they had planned. She guessed that Robert would leave it until the last moment to arrive, and she determined not to be

2

watching out for him. Nevertheless she laid her light coat and bag on the other half of the double seat to save it. Strange, but until this moment she had not doubted that he would come. It had been her own movements that had caused her concern.

He was breathless and looked anxious, but there was still five minutes before the train was due to pull out when he arrived.

'There you are darling. Such a rush I've had.' He smiled at her, and she knew his words were for the benefit of the other occupants of the open carriage. 'Here, I'll put the cases on the rack.' He swung them up, then, moving her coat to the opposite seat, 'we'll try to keep it free,' he said as he sat beside her, his face lightly touching her cheek. 'Everything all right,' he whispered. She nodded, too overcome now to speak. His hand reached for hers, 'I'll fetch us a drink when we start moving. Remember your new name?'

They were keeping their Christian names and simply changing Robert's surname from Jameson to Trebor. 'Robert the other way round so we can always work it out if we ever should forget,' he had said laughing when they discussed the idea. Then they had both discarded old diaries and address books, everything which could trace or identify them.

'We don't want to be continually looking over our shoulder, do we, my love? We'll have new contacts, make new friends, people who know us as a couple. Is there anyone you can't do this to?' he'd asked her. It had taken her a moment or two before she answered.

3

'No, but in a few weeks when we're settled I'll contact Aunt Margaret and tell her,' she said, 'but that's sufficient unto the day. There's no-one else I'm close enough to.'

The grain jerked and snorted. Robert squeezed her fingers. 'We're off Clare. No more clandestine meetings, no more guilt for either of us. I've drawn out all my money and left it in an envelope for Jean. I've enough with me to last us a few months and it's the right time of year for coastal jobs. By the end of the summer I expect I'll have sorted out something more in my own line, even if it means moving inland a bit.'

She ran her free hand through the back of her long dark hair. 'Me too Robert. The important thing is that we'll be together, whatever comes.'

The train snorted again, then suddenly they were moving, past the terminus buildings, the factories, over the river and away from London. As it gathered speed Clare watched the countryside flashing past, a lake, woods, houses, shops and pubs; communities where everyone knew each other. Now she and Robert were going into the unknown, without jobs, without anywhere to live – but with each other, 'For better or for worse…' Robert had softly said all the words of the marriage service when he had placed that ring on her finger.

'In Torquay we'll start as a married couple,' he said, 'I'm sure it will be better that way and it isn't harming anyone. I only wish I could do it for real,' he'd added quietly, 'but it makes no difference to my love for you.'

Robert went along to the buffet later and returned with two coffees, some sandwiches and two small bottles of wine. 'For a toast just before we arrive,' he said, 'OK?'

'Oh Robert.'

'That's the first time you've laughed since I boarded the train sweetheart. I thought you were having regrets already.'

'Silly. Of course not. I got them all over on the station and I'm fine now. And hungry, gosh I didn't realise how hungry until I saw that provender.'

'Here.' He passed a sandwich to her. 'Not quite the Ritz but maybe that will come.'

They opened the wine when they were twenty minutes away from their destination.

'Well darling, here's to us and our new life together. To Mr and Mrs Trebor.'

'Mr and Mrs Trebor,' she echoed quietly, and they raised their glasses to each other.

At that moment the train began to sway, and with a sudden wrenching sound, seemed to topple, and Clare found herself falling, falling into a deep black well, just as she had in her dreams over the last few weeks. The last thing she remembered was Robert clutching her and throwing his body over hers, his mouth warm and sensuous against her cheek, and his voice murmuring, 'Oh my God. Darling I love you.'

When she opened her eyes everything was still. She clambered from beneath Robert's body and she knew he was dead. Nevertheless she put her head down to see if he was breathing. How long she stayed there she did not know. Somewhere in the dim background she could hear sounds, noises, but everything was muffled, and unsteadily she rose to her feet and stumbled away to fetch help.

When she opened her eyes she saw the back of a nurse by the next bed and realised she was in hospital. She felt sore and ached and she was terribly thirsty. The nurse turned to face her bed and smiled at her. 'Feeling better?' she asked, 'would you like a cup of tea?'

'Thank you, I'd love one. Nurse, what – what happened? I'm in hospital, aren't I?'

'That's right. You were on the train that crashed.'

When the nurse left a Sister came in. 'Good, you're awake my dear. Feeling a bit tender I expect but your cuts and bruises will all heal and leave no lasting marks. While nurse is getting your tea I'll fill in a few details. First, your name?'

She opened her lips to give it but no sound came. She tried again – this was ridiculous. She must remember her name.

'I – m-my name. Sister, I can't – quite... I can't remember,' she said hesitantly, 'it'll come to me in a minute.'

Sister patted her hand reassuringly. 'Well don't worry about it now my dear. After you've drunk your tea will do. I'll come and see you later.'

When Sister and nurse had gone she sipped the hot sweet tea and tried to remember what had happened. She had been on a train, they said. What was she doing on a train? On a train to where? The cup rattled in the saucer as she painfully reached over to put it on the locker.

'Please – excuse me, but, but what hospital is this? I mean what place is it in?' she asked the lady in the bed next to her.

'Torquay.'

'Torquay. Thank you.'

She knew Torquay was in Devon but she had no idea whether she lived here, had been coming for a visit...

'My handbag,' she said aloud. Of course that would tell her who she was and where she lived, then she'd know what she was doing on the train.

'Nurse, where is my handbag please? I can't find it here.' She indicated the locker.

'I'll ask Sister.'

It seemed she didn't have a handbag with her when she was found wandering along the embankment. 'It will surface,' Sister said, 'meanwhile the doctor will be in again this evening to have a look at you.'

'But I must know who I am,' she cried, clasping her hands together and feeling the ring on her finger. 'I'm married, I've a wedding ring on. Was my husband on the train too? How bad was the crash Sister, you must tell me, please.'

They couldn't tell her because they didn't know, or so they said. Oh God, she'd got to remember. Was she travelling alone, maybe she even had a child with her?

'No,' Sister assured her when she asked, 'there were no children involved.'

She looked again at the ring. It didn't look old. Surely she would know if she was married. She must have a name, everyone had a name. And a past. You couldn't be a vacuum.

The nurse brought her another cup of tea, and shortly afterwards she fell asleep. She endeavoured not to, but it was no use, her eyes simply would not stay open.

The following day they brought her an obviously new, stone coloured handbag. She opened it eagerly but there was nothing in it to identify her. It contained a Yardley powder compact and lipstick, a brown comb, two plain white handkerchiefs and one other with daisies on. The only old item in the bag was a purse/wallet containing three hundred pounds. It was brown leather and well worn. There were no diaries, photographs, driving licence, names or addresses, and the bag itself, shoulder strap style, was the type available at most large stores.

She looked at Sister with tears in her eyes. 'Are you sure it's mine?'

'No, my dear. But it is the only one not claimed. There are also two suitcases. A blue one and a brown one I think it was, but you can see them later. Right now the best thing you can do, and I know it won't be easy, is to rest and wait. The human mind is a wonderful machine, and rest is a marvellous cure. What you are experiencing is a temporary condition, believe me. Meanwhile you suggest a name we can call you for the moment.'

If Sister had expected her to come out with her own name without thinking she was disappointed.

'I don't know. You'll h-have to do it for me.' And she covered her face with her hands and sobbed. As Sister handed her one of the handkerchiefs from the bag she said, 'How about Daisy – there are two embroidered on this, and it is a pretty name. Come now.' And she put her arm around the heaving shoulders, 'in a day or two you'll remember, or someone will enquire about you. You must have patience my dear.'

She wasn't allowed to keep the handbag and she was worried about the amount of money in it. Was it hers? If so whatever was she doing with such a large sum?

By the end of the week Daisy, as the doctors and nurses called her still could not remember her name nor anything about life before the accident. They gave her tests, they told her not to worry, then they tried different tests. Nothing happened. Her memory seemed to begin when she woke in the hospital bed and saw the nurse. That seemed strange to her, that she automatically knew about nurses and hospitals.

It was easy for them to say 'don't worry, shock plays many tricks,' but she couldn't help worrying.

She had been permitted to examine the two unclaimed suitcases and their contents, but it was a wasted effort and they had now gone to the local police station. They too contained a fair quantity of new clothes, at least one of them did. New underwear and a couple of obviously new summer dresses which appeared to be her size. The other case belonged to a man, but again there was no indication of name or address.

9

Were they travelling together? Both suitcases were new, although not a matching pair. One was dark brown with a heavy zip, the other slightly smaller and dark blue. Yet, as with the handbag the style could be seen in any large department store.

The train crash attracted only a couple of paragraphs in the national newspaper she bought in the hospital the following day.

It said that six people were killed in the crash and twenty injured, but none badly. The local paper devoted much more space to the accident, naming the victims, three of whom were from that area. It also mentioned that two of the dead had not yet been identified. Fortunately knowledge of her amnesia had not leaked outside the hospital, and for the statistics she was simply one of the twenty injured.

When she had been there a week one of the hospital doctors sat on the end of her bed and said, 'Daisy, under normal circumstances we would have discharged you by now, but until we can find out more...' He spread his hands wide. 'Now that doesn't mean that we don't think everything will fall into place soon, because we do think it will, but in our opinion you are too tensed up for it to happen at present. As you relax we believe you will remember. You see what has happened, is that a mental curtain has been lowered to shut out the memory of the crash, but because you have no head injuries at all this is a psychosomatic condition, not a physical one. It will take time but it is nothing to be afraid about.'

'It's easy for you to talk like that, doctor, and I know you are trying to reassure me, but you can't imagine what it's like. Why has no-one enquired about me? If I was travelling alone I must surely know someone, somewhere, who realised I was on that train?'

'Not necessarily. Suppose you were going on holiday. Until the day you were due back someone might only wonder why you hadn't sent a card. After two weeks I expect there will be a hue and cry for you, never fear.'

But she did fear. If she was going on holiday why hadn't she booked. True it was only May and the chances of everywhere being full were not as great as in the height of the summer, but the other aspects bothered her too. No indication anywhere of who she was. Was this deliberate? Surely, surely there would have been something – a note, an address book, a letter or diary, even a luggage label. And if the handbag was hers, three hundred pounds in cash!

The doctor was speaking again. 'I'm sorry,' she said, 'I was wool gathering, trying to work it out. What did you say?'

'There's a doctor friend of mine who has a practice in the town and he is interested in your case. He also has a spare room and is willing for you to go there for a few weeks. If you agree it would be a good arrangement because then we could keep our eye on you and it would release your bed here. Ian Humphrey and his wife are a friendly couple, with them you have the greatest chance of finding yourself quickly. Will you think about it?'

'How could I pay him? I have nothing unless the police find that the handbag is mine. And how can we prove that?'

'Not to worry about payment for the moment,' he said. 'Ian and Jill would be happy to have you stay as their guest, and we can take it one step at a time. Think of it as convalescence. I'll ask him to come in and see you tomorrow.' He smiled suddenly at her, 'Then you can size each other up.'

Ian Humphrey appeared to be in his mid-forties. He seemed shy at first, as he sat by the bed and talked to her.

'Dr Plymouth is a friend of the family,' he said, 'and if you are with us for a while he'll be able to pop in and chat, and he thinks you will relax better this way and then you'll remember who you are and what you were doing on that train. I agree with him. By the way – he tells me you are bothered about paying your way - well I can solve that one. My receptionist left a couple of weeks ago, she's expecting her baby any day, and Jill, my wife has been filling in, but frankly it's not her cup of tea. In fact, although she's been doing it willingly enough to help out she doesn't want it to become a permanent job for her.' He smiled and, and suddenly looked much younger. 'If you would like to when you are quite fit, you could release her from that job for a while.'

She lay in bed that night thinking about her future. Until her memory returned – if her memory returned, and surely, surely please God it would – everyone here seemed to think it was simply a matter of time and

12

circumstance – she had to do something and live somewhere. Perhaps it would be better to do so under the friendly doctor's umbrella.

The Humphrey household consisted of Ian, his wife Jill and their daughter, Sarah. Fifteen year old Sarah attended the local college and of them all she was the unfriendliest. Perhaps it isn't true to call her that Daisy thought when she was in bed in the very comfortable spare room that night. Ungracious certainly for she had sat and stared at Daisy for some minutes before saying, 'I've never met anyone who's lost their memory but you look all right. I can't see my father being of much help though. He's only a down to earth, common and garden doctor. Surely you need a psychiatrist.'

She had turned away, embarrassed, and Ian, as he had asked her to call him, said quickly and quite sharply, 'That will do, Sarah. Daisy doesn't want an interrogation at this time of night.'

The girl shrugged. 'I'm not very interested anyway,' she said. Later, when his daughter had gone to her room Ian apologised. 'Sorry about Sarah's attitude. It isn't really directed at you, she's like it with everyone these days.'

He looked so woebegone she felt the need to offer comfort. 'Probably a stage she's going through.'

'We hope so, don't we, Jill? But it seems to have been with us far too long. Ever since she went to college in fact, nearly a year ago now, and it doesn't seem to improve at all.'

13

'We mustn't foist our problems on to you,' Jill said, smiling across the room to her, 'but we seem to spend a lot of time apologising for our daughter lately.'

'It's okay. I expect I seem like some kind of a freak to her, a woman who's lost half her life.'

'Mislaid it,' Ian said.

'Thank you. Actually I was wondering how I knew it was a stage Sarah was going through. I mean, do you suppose I've got a daughter too?'

'Not one that age, unless you married extremely young.' Ian's grey eyes crinkled with laughter, 'More likely to remember, subconsciously, your own experiences as a teenager. You will probably find there are a lot of things you will automatically know, because you see Daisy, your brain isn't damaged, it has simply erected a divider between before and after the accident.'

'And do you think the shock of the crash caused this, or – or something bad that I don't want to remember?'

'Ah my dear, I'm not wise. As my daughter rightly said, 'I'm only a common and garden doctor,' he rose from his chair and walked across to her, 'but I do truly believe you need to give the situation a little time.'

'How much time Ian? I mean suppose, just suppose it doesn't return at all. I know you think it will, and I want to believe you. I do believe you most of the time, but I can't help that nagging doubt. What happens if my memory never comes back and no-one checks on me?'

'Well the newspapers would probably run your story.'

'You mean, does anyone know this face. That sort of thing?'

14

'Mmm.'

'No. No, - I'd - I'd hate it.'

'And I'm sure it won't be necessary. In any case if it came to that, then you could simply begin again. The important thing at this stage is also one of the hardest my dear. You know as well as I do what it is. Not to worry. Doctor Plymouth will be keeping in close touch, meanwhile a period of convalescence won't come amiss. Go out and enjoy the sea air before the promenade becomes crowded with holiday makers.'

Daisy did just that. She was loathe to at first but Jill encouraged her. 'Have a look at Torquay. Something may ring a bell. If you don't live here but in London then you could have been arriving for a holiday and perhaps that's because you know the place from previous visits.'

'I suppose you're right.'

She went onto the front at first and simply tried to enjoy the fresh sea air. It wasn't crowded and it was a mild day. She sat on a seat and after a few moments an elderly woman stopped, glanced at her, then came and sat beside her.

'You're a stranger here,' she said, 'where do you live?'

Taken by surprise at the direct question Daisy was flustered and found herself stuttering, 'I-I-in the town.' She rose quickly but the woman put out her hand.

'Don't go,' she said, 'and don't take any notice of me. I know I'm too inquisitive, but it's so nice to see a different face. I live in lodgings here all the year round and I usually have a chat with folk I meet during the day. Summer's best,' she continued, 'when all the visitors are here. The

15

place comes alive then. My name's Maudie by the way, what's yours?'

'Daisy.'

The woman held out her hand, 'Maudie Church. Glad to know you Daisy. Daisy what?'

Daisy looked towards the sea and knew her lips were trembling.

'Daisy…' her voice sounded hoarse, she almost said seashore as she took in the clean lines of the bay. 'Daisy Shore.'

'I hope – I hope we'll be friends.' Maudie looked down at Daisy's wedding ring and said, 'What does your husband do?'

She longed to tell this nosy old woman to go to hell, but the words wouldn't come and Maudie forestalled her. 'I'm sorry love. I don't mean to pry but me tongue runs away with me sometimes. It's none of my business anyway but I can't help being interested. Forget it please and say you'll be here again tomorrow. Maybe we could have a cup of tea together.'

Recovering quickly now Daisy said, 'I'm a widow and I'm here for a while to – to recuperate after an – an illness.'

Maudie touched her hand. 'Well if your lodgings or hotel gets lonely you're more than welcome to come round to me anytime. It's only one room dear but I've got me little cooker there, and me kettle.'

'Thank you, but I'm staying with friends. I have to go now…' it wasn't easy to escape from the lonely little woman and Daisy sighed as she walked slowly back. She

16

must remember to avoid that particular shelter. Tears clouded her vision as she thought yet again – if only I could remember something from before the accident. Surely soon there would be something to spark off a recollection of life before that awful moment in hospital.

Doctor Plymouth seemed strangely pleased with her when he called in the following evening.

'You are looking much better,' he said, 'sleeping well?'

'Yes, but I still can't remember anything doctor.'

'That will happen when you're least expecting it,' he answered cheerfully, 'you can't rush these things my dear. Ah, thank you Jill, that hospital tea is diabolical.'

He took the proffered drink from the tray and Jill said lightly, 'I believe you only visit us to have a decent cup of tea.'

He didn't stay long but his calm acceptance of her loss of memory situation unnerved Daisy.

'Doctor Plymouth seems to be treating me as though I'll be here forever and no-one's doing anything about trying to – to recover my – the blanks in my mind,' she said when he had left. Her cup rattled unsteadily as she replaced it in the saucer. 'It's all right for him, I'm just another patient who's not even very ill. I can walk and talk, see, hear and even think…' suddenly she covered her face with both hands and sobbed.

17

Chapter 2

Jean Jameson hurried from the kitchen to answer the telephone. Surely Philip wouldn't ring at this time of day when he knew Robert would be coming in at any moment. *Unless, unless* his wife had finally agreed to a divorce. She could believe he would throw caution to the winds then in his enthusiasm to tell her; for she had witnessed the depth of the passions he seldom allowed to surface.

In the hall she watched the front door for signs of Robert's shadow as she answered the call. 'Jean, listen darling because I've got to be quick. I've just seen Robert getting out of a taxi with a large suitcase, and hurrying into the station. I dashed back to see what was happening and he went through the barrier for the Torquay train.'

'Philip, but, are you sure it was him?'

'Positive. I've got to go now, I've no more change. I'll have another talk with...' his voice disappeared and was replaced by the long hum of sound when connections have been severed.

Slowly she returned to the kitchen and automatically turned the oven down. Did this mean Robert had left her? Gone to this woman he wanted to marry? Philip may have been mistaken, although he was a meticulous man and he'd been *very* sure. Yet what use would it be if Robert left her, and Philip's wife still refused to divorce him. The only way she'd let Robert go, was if Philip was free to marry *her*, and that didn't look like coming off. It was easy for him to say he'd talk to his wife again, and she believed he did his best, but doubtless she too had her reasons. Probably the same as mine, she thought - hanging on to status, to respectability, even in this day and age. Maybe if I was eighteen I wouldn't think like this, but I'm twenty eight and, yes, maybe I'm a bit prim too. Robert always says so. She thought about it as she went round the house, straightening cushions that hardly needed it, shifting an ornament to a different angle. What determines a person's outlook? Apart from their genes - was it their background? Hers had been very proper, and possibly rather narrow. She often wondered if it was the contrast in their natures that had led to her falling in love with Robert in the first place. Philip now was so different - she understood him.

Jean had never wanted to know more than was absolutely necessary about Philip's wife. 'I don't want to think about her as a person,' she had said to him, 'just as a statistic blocking the way to our marriage. If she would divorce you, then I'd accede to Robert's wishes and he could marry *his* girlfriend.'

God, what a mess. But no way was she putting her future in jeopardy for a dream. She loved Philip, but if he wasn't free then they either carried on as they were, or said goodbye forever. She knew that would be the hardest decision to make, but she would make it if it came to that. She had worked too long with solicitors in that particular department not to know the pitfalls. She never intended to be one of the wives pleading for more money, nor yet one who finished up without rights. All the while she stayed Robert's wife she had entitlements...

19

the sound of a car sent her hurrying into the lounge at the front of the house, but it was simply one travelling down the road.

She looked at the clock. Robert was late. But surely he wouldn't go without telling her. He'd asked often enough for a divorce, had he really taken matters into his own hands now and was he on a train to - where did Philip say, Torquay?

Perhaps he intended travelling a couple of stations and telephoning her from a hotel somewhere to frighten her into agreeing. Drawing her lips together she seemed to gather all her resources tighter; if *that* was their game, Robert and his fancy woman, then they'd lose that one too - unless Philip became free. It would certainly be a different story then.

Twenty minutes later Jean took the casserole from the oven, put away one of the plates, and dished herself a reasonable helping. Carrying it into the dining room where the table was set for two, she poured herself a glass of red wine, and solemnly ate her dinner. She was alert to every sound outside, even leaving the curtains drawn back, which was very unusual when they were having a meal. Several cars went by - none turned into the drive.

She found the note when she went upstairs to bed. It was eleven o'clock then, and she was sure that Philip was right and Robert had finally left. If he hadn't seen him going into the station with a suitcase she would have been onto the police by now, or even checking the hospitals herself; but from the time of his call she had

20

known really that Robert wasn't coming back. Philip didn't make mistakes of that kind - maybe that's why we are friends as well as lovers, she thought, because we think along the same lines, are both such logical and sensible people.

It had been over for her and Robert a long time now - certainly before she met Philip, and she felt sure before Robert met whoever his girlfriend was. Neither of them mentioned names when they discussed the situation, it was always, in his case, 'Because I want to marry again.'

The large brown envelope was lying on her pillow. He must have returned to the house and left it there whi e she was at work. Glancing across to the other single bed in the room, *Robert's bed*, the thought flitted very quickly through her mind that now Philip could spend the night here sometimes if they were careful and he could get away.

Without haste she picked the envelope up. It was quite fat, but she could no more have torn it open immediately than she ever did with birthday or Christmas gifts. Always she went for the scissors and the waste basket to put the wrapping in. Few things hurt by keeping was her maxim. Robert usually laughed - he would have torn it open regardless. She went downstairs for the letter opener.

The amount of money in the envelope amazed her. She knew of course that he would not leave her destitute, but he must have drawn every penny from his account... he knew she had hers too, with a good salary paid into it each month, so it was a *very* generous gesture. For a few

21

seconds she thought back to the beginning, all those years ago when they were in love. He was quite the handsomest man she had met then, and his buoyant, outgoing nature *had* thrilled her. He'd made her feel important and he was always generous. Flowers, chocolates, the best seats at the theatre, even after they married and during those first few months when she lost the baby and had to give up her job. He wasn't in such an exalted position then and they couldn't really afford them, but... *live for today* was his motto then, and when that *'first fine careless rapture'*, had flown it was his generosity, strangely enough, that annoyed her most.

She was still holding the notes, and as she now flicked quickly through them she realised there was several thousand pounds there. Questions tumbled over each other in her neat mind. How would he live? Was his girlfriend rich? He had a good job in management, had he obtained another post somewhere with a huge salary? Or was he planning to kill himself and never need money again?

She dismissed the last thought as soon as it was formed. Robert's conscious would insist he did the right thing by her. Well she too would make certain he did - and that meant she would stay his wife until it suited her not to do so. In five years' time of course he would be able to insist on divorce, but that was sufficient unto the day.

Laying the money on the blue satin eiderdown, she opened the folded sheet of white notepaper that was with it. 'Jean, I've tried everything I can to do this thing

22

amicably. All I want is my freedom. I *know* I shall be happy, I hope you will too. The money is in lieu of alimony because I can soon make some more. Good luck, Robert.'

For a moment her eyes clouded over. How typical of the man. No grudges, and generous to the end. Because it *was* the end now. Jean knew he would never return. She would have to invent a story to explain his absence. It would never do to let the neighbours think he had left her. Rustling the note between her thumb and fingers she sat there on the edge of the bed making her plans.

By the morning she had her story ready. She would tell people that Robert had left his firm for a better job, but it involved him being out of England for a year. Originally she thought two or three years, but discarded that in favour of one year, which sounded reasonable.

Her reasons for not going with him were because she had such a good post here herself, and he would be very busy, leaving her with little to do. His destination caused a bit of a problem. If she had him in Europe people would expect him to fly home occasionally, and if she sent him into the bush or the jungle somewhere it wouldn't tie in with his job, and she didn't want to alter that. Eventually she settled for Australia. Melbourne itself, which she could read up, and pretend the information came from his letters. And as it was so far away detection must be less. Robert would be working for an English firm setting up an office there, then there'd be no legal complications with regard to salary and tax.

Her parents, living in Spain since their early retirement, need not know what had happened, and her

23

correspondence with her sister in Scotland was always sketchy, and they hadn't met since her wedding. It never once crossed her mind, during that long and rather painful night, to speak the truth. Rather, a slow anger lit a fire that was still smouldering in the morning. That Robert could put her to this *indignity* was outrageous. But no-one except Philip, would know he had left her, and she would not try to find him. He was gone and she had her story mapped out. She was the one in limbo now, and it was a nasty feeling.

She divided the money into bundles. She would bank a hundred pound a month - that would look reasonable to everyone, bank manager and clerk alike. Tearing Robert's note into minute fragments, without rereading it, she placed all the money in the tin box where they kept insurance policies and other legal documents. Then she tried to sleep.

Philip did not immediately return home after telephoning Jean. 'Come along Writ,' he said to the airdale at his side, 'let's walk a bit more - I need to think.'

If Robert *had* gone off, Jean would undoubtedly put the pressure on. The worst part of their relationship for her was, he knew, the fact that she had no legal status, no rights. Love was enough for some people, it never would be for her. He knew *he* could have carried on as they were. Not ideal, but it isn't an ideal world, he often told himself, and mistakes have to be paid for. His marriage was a mistake - not only for him, but for Sonia too. A blessing there were no children. That at least was one thing they had agreed about. Her own experiences as a

24

child had made her vulnerable and there would have been no chance of release if they'd had a family. As things were it didn't seem likely she would agree, but it was perhaps worth another try.

I do want to marry Jean, to be with her all the time, he thought as he strode along, the dog by his side. But there's no denying I've felt safe all the while Robert was still there. As though the matter didn't rest with me - it was circumstances, and there was nothing I could do. Now, *I don't know*. I love Jean more than I've ever loved anyone in my life, but it's no use ruining my career, that wouldn't help either of us, and she'd be the first to acknowledge the fact. It will be a nasty business anyway, but the more low key we can keep it the easier it will be for all of us.

He let Writ off the lead again in the park, and walked on deep in thought while the dog ran ahead, then back, and covered the ground three times to his master's once. Illogically he thought, I hope Sonia won't want to keep Writ - I should miss him so. Then he smiled a little to himself at the way his mind was working. He was presuming she would eventually agree to divorce him.

'Come on Writ, time to head back boy. You've had a bonus tonight, and I don't think I'm any closer to solving my problem than I was before we set out.' He attached the dogs lead, and walked briskly out of the park and into the busy street.

25

Chapter 3

Daisy avoided the park for fear of meeting Maudie. She felt rather mean about it, for the little woman was probably harmless in normal circumstances. Simply very lonely, well she knew all about that, for what could be lonelier than her situation now. A stranger in a familiar world, for it was true she did remember, subconsciously, how to live. She never had to think about procedure or customs, she automatically did the correct thing.

Her cuts and bruises had healed and one evening she broached the subject of work to Ian and Jill. Sarah was out and they had sat over the dinner table as the setting sun cast a golden path by the window and across the garden. Ian drank the last of the wine in his glass before replying.

'You mean as my receptionist, Daisy?'

She nodded. 'If the job is still going, and if you think I would be suitable.'

'Oh yes, I only hesitate because I don't want you to rush it. But if you feel fit enough then it's fine with me. And with you, isn't it Jill?' He smiled at his wife.

'I'll be glad to get back to my sewing room,' she said. They agreed the financial side, and in spite of her protests that she was keen to begin by learning the ropes from Jill immediately, Ian won the day for her to have until the end of the week free, and it was settled that she would start work on Monday morning. She retired that night happy in the knowledge that soon she would be earning a wage and have something definite to do for the rest of the day. This vacuum of not knowing was terrifying. She had tried Jill's old typewriter only the other day, although Jill said she probably wouldn't need it because the job was mostly keeping the appointment diary, filing notes, answering the telephone, and knowing the patients.

'We haven't aspired to a computer yet,' she said laughing, 'we are still steam operated. Just as well Daisy,' she continued when she watched her efforts at hunt and peck. 'You obviously didn't earn your living as a typist.'

The two women had become friends, and perhaps only Jill could have made her laugh with such a remark. With Ian she found it hard to be light hearted about her dilemmas. She didn't feel light hearted about it anyway, but with Jill she was unembarrassed by the gaps in her memory.

Sarah tolerated her and it showed. But as Ian had pointed out, this was her attitude to everyone, certainly everyone who came to the house, and she was often abominably rude to her parents. This was something Jill could unburden to her, the hurts she sustained by her daughter's manner, and Daisy felt she was helping a little by listening.

'You have a lovely understanding nature,' Jill said, 'and you're full of grace. The way you walk, the way you talk. I think you probably did a caring job once.'

Of course, she thought, it's all conjecture, but she could discuss possibilities like this with Jill. What good it was she didn't know, because no matter how hard she concentrated there seemed to be nothing before that

27

frightening moment in the hospital when Sister asked her name.

That was another thing, she didn't know how old she was. She realised it was silly to worry over something like that, yet she couldn't help it. It mattered to her whether she was twenty, thirty, or whatever. Not even to Jill had she voiced this particular despair, which was beginning to have a nightmarish hold on her. It will be good to have a proper job to do, apart from the financial independence she thought, if it gives me less time to niggle at who I am and where I come from.

On Sunday evening Jill and Ian went out for a drink. They invited her but she excused herself on the pretext of 'preparing for work, and writing up my journal.' The journal was begun on Ian's advice as something definite to do. She recorded unexciting incidents of her doings in the hope that something, sometime, might ring a bell to her past. She heard Sarah go out soon after her parents, and an hour later the door crashed with a velocity that made her jump. She rushed into the hall, and Sarah was halfway up the stairs.

'My goodness, you nearly gave me a heart attack,' she said.

'Oh *very funny*. I do still happen to live here you know. Anyway why aren't you out with my parents?'

Taken by surprise she stuttered slightly, 'Well I – I h-had things to do.' Sarah's unblinking and defiant stare caused her to add, 'I wanted to wash my hair and write some letters.'

'Write some letters. Hur. I thought you were a woman without a past, a lonely lost soul who needs *care and attention*.' She said care and attention as though she were quoting from a book, 'so who do you know to write to?'

Suddenly, to her dismay, Daisy couldn't prevent tears. They filled her eyes and ran down her cheeks. Turning, she stumbled back into the sitting room.

'Daisy I'm sorry. Really I am. I didn't realise it would hurt so much,'

She heard Sarah's words and slowly looked up. The girl was standing by the settee, and she put her hand out. 'It must be awful, not knowing I mean. That was a terrible thing to say, but I didn't think. I just wanted to – well, hit out at someone I guess.'

'It's all right, Sarah. After all I have rather barged into your family. I don't blame you for being resentful.'

'But I'm *not*, not really, although it probably seems that way. It's just that you seem so, well so in tune with them all the time.' She sat down beside her. 'It wasn't you I was getting at. I had such a miserable evening and I just wanted to come back and chuck things about, and you were there, I guess a ready target for my bad temper.'

'So you chucked words instead. I feel like that against the doctors sometimes. Not your father, but at the hospital I often want to shake the truth out of them and scream, "Will I ever remember who I am and what I was doing on the train?" They take it so calmly, metaphorically patting me on the head and saying, "Don't worry, it will

29

return someday I expect," and never seeing what a huge mountain it is to climb from my view.'

Tentatively she reached out and touched Sarah's hand. 'Shall I make some coffee?' she said.

It was a turning point, certainly as far as Sarah was concerned. They drank their coffee and talked frankly and sincerely about their problems.

'I know I'm often unbearable,' Sarah said, 'and I hate myself for it, but somehow...'

'It is sometimes hard to explain to others,' Daisy said.

'See tonight I was with a crowd from college, but I thought I was going to be with a special guy. We were going to clear off and leave the others, and, and he *ignored* me. Spent all the time chatting up one of the others.' She lifted her head defiantly, 'So I walked out,' she choked, 'and he – he *laughed*. I could hear him as I reached the door...'

Daisy put her arm round the girl's now heaving shoulders,

'I'm sorry. I'm not usually a cry baby Daisy, but I really got hooked on this guy see.'

Sarah had gone to her room by the time her parents returned and Daisy was reading a book.

She woke early on Monday morning, conscious that she was at last making a definite effort to begin a new life. Doctor's receptionist – at least it would give her a background. Wearing a smart, light blue linen dress, one from the case which the police had now released to her on Ian's assumption that as everything in it was her size, and no-one else had claimed it, she must be the owner.

He had gone with her to collect that and the handbag. He did most of the talking. 'It still upsets Mrs Shore so much to discuss that day,' he said. He had already been to the police station to, as he put it, sort it out for her, and whatever reason he gave for there not being any identification in either the handbag or the suitcase, must have satisfied them, for they did not mention it; only insisted that they actually handed the items to her. Some day she would ask him, but not yet.

Nervously she went into the surgery buildings with Ian that Monday morning. The work wasn't difficult and by the end of the session Daisy had a good grip of where everything was and a list of procedures. Ian suggested she take the afternoon off because evening surgery didn't begin until five and the telephone could be switched through to the house meantime. Nevertheless she was back in her little office just after four, 'because if I'm completely familiar with the system everything will continue to run smoothly,' she said, 'and I would like to read some of the medical magazines too if I may?'

Ian laughed, 'You certainly believe in doing a job properly,' he said, 'I can see I'll need to watch out or you'll be treating the patients next.'

The evening surgery was lighter than the morning one, and she felt she coped quite well with the personal questions the patients asked. Where did she live, where had she worked before, and, looking at her wedding ring one extrovert and rather noisy woman who couldn't seem to control her own small son from tearing round and

31

making a great nuisance of himself, 'How many children have you got, Mrs Shore?'

'I haven't any children,' she said, in what she hoped was a calm voice, 'and I'm a widow.'

At least they all knew something about her now, even if it wasn't the truth. The very nature of the situation should stop further questions about her past, she thought, when someone had hauled the woman's child down yet again from trying to swing on the mantelpiece. Quickly she flipped through the cards for the noisy woman's name. Thank goodness she was next but one in to see Ian.

Giving herself a past to share with the world helped, but it didn't alleviate the isolation she experienced when she was alone. It was all very well for Doctor Plymouth to say, however kindly, 'Don't think about it because that isn't the way your memories will return. Make new friends, enjoy your work and one day, probably quite out of the blue, you will recall. I'm sure of it. It's not a bang on the head that brings these things back you know, it's time – a healing time.'

Desperately as she wanted her before the train crash self to return she was also frightened of it. Suppose she had been an evil woman, a cruel mother, or daughter, a wicked wife. She tried hard to shut out these thoughts, seldom succeeding. Hinting at them to Jill one afternoon, her friend said quietly, 'You weren't any of those things Daisy for the simple reason that it would show now if you were. We all sometimes do or say unkind things, who is perfect after all? But you were, and are, no more wicked

32

than I am, I'd stake my reputation as a good character reader on that.'

Daisy laughed, but her heart wasn't in it. Later Jill came into the garden with the local paper in her hand, 'Would you like to come to the ballet with me on Saturday, Daisy? There's no surgery Saturday evening, and it's a company I've seen before. They're excellent.'

'What about Ian?'

'Ian *hates* ballet. Says he can never follow the story, but I love it. Do say you'll come.'

It felt good to dress up, Daisy thought, as she zipped herself into a deep pink frock which was obviously new. That had to be her case for not only did the garments fit, but the styles suited her. She twirled around, letting the full skirt swing out and fall back into soft folds. It was made of a georgette type material, had a cowl neckline and long sleeves culminating in a gathered cuff. A honeymoon dress, she thought, her mind desperately seeking a link with the girl in the crash. If that were so, who was her bridegroom?

'Daisy, we leave in twenty minutes, that all right with you?' Jill's voice outside the door cut into her thoughts.

'Yes, fine,' she called back, 'I'm almost ready now.'

The theatre was on the seafront, and Ian drove them there, checked the time the performance finished and said he would return for them then.

'Saves parking problems and means I've got the car in case of emergencies,' he said, adding, as he helped her out, 'You're looking especially beautiful this evening Daisy. Isn't she Jill?'

33

Mingling with the crowd going in Daisy felt a surge of excitement. 'I'm so looking forward to this,' she whispered, touching Jill's arm.

'Me too Daisy. Ballet isn't Ian's scene and I'm such a balletomaniac that I come anyway, but I would much rather have a companion.'

Daisy read the programme avidly. In fact so engrossed was she that when the lights went down and the music began it startled her. Everything slotted into place, yet she remembered nothing definite. Only that it all seemed familiar. She found herself thinking in terms of dance, noting technical details that convinced her she must have been in the profession. Suppressing her excitement as best she could she said to Jill during the interval, 'Do I look like a ballet dancer to you? Or a teacher,' she added quickly.

'Yes. You have the fluidity of movement, a flowing line when you walk. Have you remembered something Daisy?' Jill didn't try to hide *her* excitement.

'Not really remembered, but I know it all. I mean, I knew what the next steps were going to be and… it's starting again, we'll have to talk later.'

The déjà vu feeling she had experienced went on all evening, but when they were leaving the theatre Daisy said, almost apologetically, 'Jill, I would rather you didn't say anything to Ian yet if you don't mind. I'd like to, to think about it a bit first.'

'Of course you would. I won't breathe a word my dear. The last thing you need now is a lot of questions fired at you, I can see that; but don't leave him too long.'

34

Back home Daisy was impatient to go to her room, but she stayed and had a night-cap with Ian and Jill. When she did reach her bedroom she closed the door quietly and leaned against it, breathing hard. It was the oddest feeling, this knowledge that she knew about the world of ballet. Kicking off her shoes she tentatively tried some steps.

That's it, she thought, I was in the entertainment world, a dancer or a teacher. She tried again, lightly pirouetting round the bed, then she placed the straight-backed chair in the centre of the room and used it as a bar for limbering up.

If only she could remember. Obviously she had something to do with ballet, in the chorus most probably, for if she had been well known someone would surely have tried to find her. Perhaps she had no family, yet she must have lived *somewhere*, known *someone*. It was three months since the train crash, if anyone had been worried over her they would have come forward by now. More and more Daisy was of the opinion that she had indeed been alone in the world. At least as far as relations and close friends were concerned.

In spite of her desire to keep her thoughts to herself about the little jog of memory, she felt so mean at not telling her benefactor that a couple of days later she did so. He took the news calmly. What had she expected – that he would be as over the moon as she was?

'That's very good Daisy. It gives you a lead, and I fully expect the rest of your memory to return within the next few months now it has started.'

35

Daisy tried hard to remember during the next few days, but eventually gave up and settled down to the idea that this was something one just could not rush. She concentrated wholeheartedly on her job, and she began to enjoy it.

She met Maude Church, her companion from the seafront when she was on the promenade one morning, gazing over the rails and wondering about the lives of everyone on the beach. Maude tapped her on the shoulder and she spun round so quickly that the older woman apologised.

'I didn't mean to startle you luv. I'm so glad to see you again. How about coming for a cup of tea, there's a nice little café opposite here. I often go in there.'

Over a pot of tea they talked. Maude, it seemed, had had a raw deal in life, looking after her ailing and elderly parents while her own children were growing up, and never really having enough money to not worry about being able to pay the bills. Then being widowed six months after the last parent died. 'Just planning all the things we'd try an' do when he was taken bad. I nursed him of course, but – I guess it wasn't meant to be for us to gallivant.

'Three kids I had luv. Billy, the middle one, he died when he was seven. Pneumonia the doctor said it was, but 'ed allus been frail like. I think I always knew, deep down, that he'd not make old bones. It was awful that, c'os you hope, don't you? Even when things look black.' She looked skywards. 'He often helps me, mind. Bet he's a nice lad now. Best looking one of the lot 'e was.'

36

The eldest boy had gone to Australia when he was twenty, and the youngest child, Maudie's daughter, married a Norwegian.

'Lives out there in the land of the midnight sun. She sent me a picture postcard of it once. Beautiful. I might make it there to see her one day,' her voice was wistful for only a couple of seconds then she grinned, 'an' I might not. There's a lot of England I've not seen yet without going to foreign parts for all I'd love to see her again. What about you luv? You getting on all right?'

Just in time Daisy remembered she had told Maude she was a widow. 'Yes, yes thank you. Beginning to find my feet,' she said.

'You were staying with friends when we talked before. Don't disappear without letting me know will you? I like you. There's something, I don't quite know how to put this, but something vulnerable about you. Don't take too much notice of me luv. My Jack used to say as how I saw things that weren't there.'

'Actually I'm, I'm settling here for a bit. I'm working now as a doctors receptionist, so I'll be around for a while Maudie.'

She was pleased she could communicate now without that terrible panic that assailed her at first. Perhaps it's because I'm beginning to remember, she thought, although you could hardly call these vague familiarities remembrance. Yet it gave her confidence that her past really was still there, "lurking behind the curtain in her mind" is how Ian described it.

37

Nevertheless she often became very impatient with herself, and it was on one of these occasions that Sarah made her suggestion. They had all finished their meal and Sarah left the room to go upstairs when the telephone rang. She took the call, then they heard her go upstairs and bang the door.

Ian sighed. 'It's incredible how that girl has changed from the co-operative child, well *fairly* co-operative child, to an almost unmanageable teenager,' he said. 'If we complain too much about her behaviour she slams out of the house and that's even worse, not knowing where she is or who she's with…'

Later Daisy went to her room. 'Have to fill in my diary,' she said to them, smiling. 'That was a good idea Ian, and it's turning me into an author. I'm often tempted to go on and make up the bits I don't know, but so far I've resisted the urge. I may start another notebook though, and try writing a story one day.'

She liked to escape to her room sometimes during the evening to give Ian and Jill time alone together. Living with them as one of the family was working well, but she knew it couldn't go on for ever. Luckily it was a large house, with several reception rooms so if any of them wanted privacy it was possible.

She had been in her room for a few moments only when Sarah tapped on the door. 'Daisy, I've had an idea,' she said, without preamble. 'About your memory.'

Daisy swallowed hard. Sometimes Sarah's bluntness left her feeling absolutely defenceless. 'Come and sit down and – and tell me,' she said.

'That 'phone call just now. It was from my friend whose mum runs a dancing school. Only a small one, but she's short staffed at the moment because her only assistant is off sick. Debbie, my friend, she's an ace pianist and she's having to stay and help out by playing for them. Now what I was wondering is why don't you see if she'd like to employ you until her proper teacher returns?'

'I don't think –'

'*Why not, Daisy?* It could be the opening you're looking for. We know you can dance, and obviously you had something to do with ballet dancers or you wouldn't know all you do about them,' she shrugged her shoulders and tried to look nonchalant. 'I'm being selfish really, because if you were to offer your services it would release Debbie. I hate kicking my heels like this every night.'

'I don't know if I can play the piano.'

'But you could teach dancing.' In spite of what she called her selfish motives, Sarah sounded excited. 'And you want to get your memory back, don't you? Well forget what my father and old Plymouth at the hospital say about waiting and it will all come to you. You've got to take what you can I reckon, and once you are back in an environment we're all sure you were used to, it will give your memory cells or whatever they are a much better chance.'

Daisy promised to think about it, and indeed she thought of little else for the rest of the evening, but it was several days later when she broached the subject to Ian. Sarah hadn't mentioned it again because she had hardly been home, having taken up playing tennis with another friend during the absence of Debbie.

'Won't do any harm and it may do good,' Ian said, 'how do you feel about it?'

'I'm not sure but I think I would like to try.'

That night it was Daisy who knocked on Sarah's door to tell her she would like to offer her services as an assistant in her friend's mother's dancing school. 'I shall have to tell her the truth, Sarah, that I haven't any qualifications that I know of. And, and about my amnesia.'

In a surprisingly gentle voice Sarah said, 'That's all right. I'll tell her and make an appointment for you at the same time. I'll let you know tomorrow.'

The first afternoon she went to assist at the ballet school she felt extremely nervous. Pam Greenfield, who ran the small school, seemed friendly and was certainly grateful. They had worked out her hours to fit in with her job at the surgery. She was to help with the afternoon class each day, and the evening one for older children on the night there was no evening surgery.

The classes were held in Pam's house, a rambling, Victorian villa where the whole of the lower floor had been converted into the school. Toilets, washbasins, changing rooms, and three reasonably sized rooms knocked into one for the hall. There was even a small stage at one end, 'so the children can practise in a smaller area and become used to working within the confines of a stage,' Pam told her.

The afternoon class was the pre-school children, and Daisy was surprised how many attended. Her nervousness left her as she began teaching, listening to Pam's instructions to the children and helping them get it right. Pam played the piano, half swung round on the stool to watch their progress.

When the class finished she helped some of them to change, finding shoes and hairbrushes, and chatting to the mums, a few dads, and several grandparents who had come to collect their progeny. One little girl was alone, sitting right at the end of the bench and struggling to do up her black patent shoes. Daisy went to help and smiled to herself as she noticed the child's cardigan buttoned up one hole out all the way.

'Your cardi's all lopsided,' she laughed softly as she unbuttoned it and started again. When she had straightened the offending garment and buttoned the shiny shoes she stood up to find a tall young man hovering near.

'You ready Alison?' He turned to Daisy. 'Thank you. I'm a bit late collecting her today. Got held up.' His voice was deep and bit gruff. 'Come on.' He jerked the child to her feet and strode off down the corridor with her.

'Hm. You did well to get a word out of Julien Uppark.' Pam joined her and together they checked the bench for left over clothes. 'He usually grabs Alison's hand and makes off as if he's kidnapping her. Think he's embarrassed coming in to collect her when all the others are so much older than him. Hope you enjoyed it this afternoon because you'll be OK here, I can see that.'

'I did. I really did, Pam.'

Daisy returned to Murray House with a happier heart than she had experienced since the train crash.

Chapter 4

'I've brought something to show you, Jean,' Philip said one evening a week after Robert had left her. They were sitting in one of their favourite restaurants, Philip as usual having told his wife he was going to his photography club. The newspaper he pulled from his jacket pocket was neatly folded into a small oblong. 'There,' he said pointing his finger to a couple of paragraphs, 'I think it's about Robert.'

Jean read it steadily. She had always had immense control over her feelings, something she knew Philip appreciated and Robert found disconcerting. Nevertheless her stomach seemed to be churning around like an electric mixer as she read:

"*There are two unidentified victims from last week's train crash near Torquay. Both men, one in his sixties, white haired and wearing a dark grey suit, the other in his thirties, fair haired and blue-eyed. The older man had recently had new dentures, and the younger has an unusual shaped birthmark on his left shoulder. Police are anxious to hear from anyone who may be able to identify them.*"

'I'll have to get in touch, won't I? There couldn't be two men with that strange birthmark in the same place. And you saw him at the station."

Philip reached across the table and laid his hand over hers. 'Would you like me to come with you my dear?'

'I'll - I'll 'phone them first. I - I have to think about it Philip. I mean, as his wife I'll be expected to know where he was going. And why?'

'Yes, of course.'

In the silence she felt he must surely hear her thumping heart. Her thoughts seemed to be going wild. She wished she had seen that paper first, it would have given her *time* to work things out. Robert - dead - unidentified in a train crash - it didn't make sense.

'How about telling them he went to Torquay on business for a few days. No, for a week, that will sound better. And, and perhaps you could say you were to be away at the same time - somewhere else?'

She looked across the table into Philip's wide grey eyes. It was as though he was willing her to think along those lines, gently guiding her thoughts, and it worked.

'Yes,' she said, slowly at first, then as her mind refocused, 'And when he didn't arrive home I expected a message any time, then I saw about the train crash.'

'Mmm.' Philip inclined his head. 'And you got in touch with them immediately...'

'Think that will work. I don't want to say he'd left me but I know the police. In my job I have to, and they'll probe. Oh ever so gently if they think I'm the grieving widow, but they'll probe nonetheless. I wonder why they don't know who he is. I mean, surely he had *some* proof of identity on him.'

'May have been deliberate, you know, beginning a new life. Or it may have been damaged beyond recognition, or scattered over the Devon countryside...'

44

'Don't,' she said unexpectedly. 'He w-was my husband after all, and while I want to marry you and shall shed no tears for his departure, I - I didn't wish him dead Philip. No - no...'

She telephoned the police from the booth in the restaurant foyer. Philip stood outside, waiting and watching. It was a brief call - and she was dry eyed and in absolute control when she came out.

'They want me to go down and look. I said I'd go tomorrow. Take the day off work.'

'Wednesday. I'll come with you. I can arrange it, don't worry.'

True to his word he called for her early the following morning and they set off for Torquay. Both were silent for the first half hour, then she said, 'Philip, it is dear of you to do this. You realise that if it *is* Robert then I shall be free. Completely free. I - I suppose I'll be a widow because no-one will know he had left, will they?'

'Probably not. Except his girlfriend. Unless she too died. There were several killed I remember. If she lived, she will know the truth Jean.'

'But there's nothing she can do about it. Robert was my husband and officially I will be his widow. Those are *facts*, Philip, and nothing can alter them. That is, of course, if the body we are going to see is his.'

She was silent again, but her mind was active. Why did they not know who he was? He must have had *some* papers on him. His diary, driving licence, a name and address on something in his wallet? That part seemed a complete mystery, because he wasn't running away from

45

anything. He'd left her a note so she wasn't likely to have him listed as a missing person...

'Sorry Philip, what did you say?'

'Only asked if you wanted to stop for a break at the next service station.'

'I'd rather get on and get this thing over with, unless you...'

'No. The sooner we sort it out the better. Then you'll know where you stand. We're about halfway there now.'

Torquay was bathed in early spring sunshine. It was a place Jean had never visited before, but Philip had. 'As a child I came twice on holiday with my parents,' he told her. 'I remember having rides on a donkey, and going to a theatre perched high on a cliff. Strange memories to have of a place, but then I couldn't have been very old.'

They reached their destination by lunchtime and went to a pub for a meal. Jean refused an alcoholic drink, but lit a cigarette while they were waiting.

'Haven't smoked for four years,' she said, 'but I bought a packet early this morning. Weak of me... of course it might not be Robert.'

'That's true, but I saw him go through the barrier for that train, the one that crashed, I've since checked the time, so we *do* know he was on it. We also know he had left you, which ties in with the fact that the police don't know who he is. He may have been travelling under a false name which they have realised. I think you have to be prepared for some close questioning darling.'

46

'Yes, you're right. Well I'm ready. We'll say that you are a very close friend of the family and have come with me under that guise, shall we?'

'Good idea. I think this is our meal coming now.'

They had no difficulty identifying Robert. Jean turned away quickly, and Philip put his arm round her shoulder. He nodded to the policeman who had accompanied them, and the mortuary attendant replaced the cover. It was over in seconds, and they returned to the police station to fill in the details.

The main puzzle from the police point of view was why he had no identification on him. Jean said she couldn't answer that one. Her husband had been coming to Torquay on business - she never discussed his work with him she told them. She stayed dry eyed, but clasped her handkerchief in her hand and screwed it into a tiny ball while they softly questioned her about his job and hobbies. Philip stood by, watching her concernedly for a while then cutting in to say, 'Look is this absolutely necessary. Mrs. Jameson is trying to keep calm under the sadness of knowing it is her husband back there...'

'Only one more thing sir. What type of case did your husband have when he left home Mrs. Jameson?'

The question threw her for a moment. 'Why - why an ordinary suitcase I - I suppose. I mean, I was away, I told you. I went to look after a sick friend for a week - we, we should have arrived home within a day or so of each other.' She looked down and sniffed into her rolled up hankie, longing now for this to be over, and willing herself

47

not to think about any of it until they were on their way back home.

A constable was sent to fetch the suitcase that was still unclaimed. 'Do you recognise it Mrs. Jameson?'

She nodded. 'It's the one he takes to conferences.'

'It appears to be new. Are you sure it is your husband's? Perhaps you'd better check the contents.'

Her overwhelming thought had been to get out of here now, but she looked when the case was opened for her. She didn't touch any of the clothes, but it gave her time to think of an answer.

'Robert did buy a new one recently. His was very shabby.' She turned to smile sadly at the police officer. 'I - I had - temporarily forgotten you know, but yes, it's his.'

She was asked to sign for it, and Philip took it from the officer. 'I'll see to it,' he said.

'How much money did your husband usually take to conferences Mrs. Jameson?'

'Difficult to say. Quite - a lot.'

'A thousand pounds?'

She should have been expecting it, but she wasn't, and she knew it showed in her face. 'If - if that's what he had on him. He could have been planning to buy something - a large piece of equipment you know.'

'I would have thought it normal to pay by cheque - however, the money was in his inside jacket pocket. I'll have to ask you to sign for this too of course.'

The sun had gone in when they emerged from the police station. Philip fussed her into the car and drove

48

away. He found a parking place near the seafront and pulled in.

'Would you like to stay for a bit instead of driving straight back. A walk might do us both good,' he said.

She buttoned her coat and pulled a headscarf from the side of her handbag. 'The police thought it odd he had absolutely nothing on him for identification, didn't they, Philip?'

'And a thousand pounds in cash. Expect they're checking with M15 right now.' His attempt at light heartedness fell on deaf ears.

'I think they guessed he'd left me. That's *humiliating*.'

There was a light breeze coming from the sea, and quite a lot of people strolling along the promenade. They walked side by side, each lost in thought. After a few moments she said quietly, 'We'd fallen out of love and I was preventing him marrying this other woman, but I didn't wish him any harm Philip. I didn't want him to die. Do you suppose there's something macabre about me trying to hang on when there was nothing there anymore?'

'Of course not. It's what Sonia's doing too. I can't pretend to understand why - it's different in each case I reckon.'

'I wasn't *jealous* of *her* - this woman he went away with, and if you and I could have been together I wouldn't have even stood in her way. I wonder if she died too? It was hardly the sort of thing I could ask the police. Strange isn't it. I don't even know her name?'

49

They left Torquay an hour later. 'We'll stop in a while and have a cup of tea darling, and when we get back I'll help you with the obituary notice for the paper. That way everyone will know Robert is dead and there'll be no awkward questions.'

'What about - your wife?'

'I'll 'phone her and say I've been held up. She's used to that.'

When they stopped she looked at him across the table and said, 'It will seem odd to be free Philip. I wish it hadn't happened like that. To think that only a few days ago I was concocting a story to account for his absence. Sometimes truth is truly stranger than fiction.'

'Had you actually told anyone?'

'No. That's the remarkable thing. At work no-one knew he wasn't there of course, and with being out all day we mostly only see the neighbours at weekends. Not always then. Sometimes go weeks with no more than a wave as we go in and out.'

'What about his car?'

'His car. My God I hadn't thought of that.'

'Where is it? I mean, did he take it to the office the day he - left?'

'Of course.' Her reply was sharp. 'I suppose it's still in the office carpark. Though come to think about it, they haven't rung me to ask why he isn't at work. And if his car *is* there...'

'It probably isn't. He could have sold it to give himself some extra cash - and he must have accounted for his absence in some way or they would have been on to you by now.'

'I suppose so. Perhaps he gave up his job. It was certainly a well-planned operation; and you know of the two of us I was always the planner. Robert liked doing things on the spur of the moment.'

Philip touched her hand. 'How long were you married to him Jean?'

'Six years. But it went wrong very quickly. We were really only happy for six months, if that. We did try for the first year or two you know, both of us, then, well we went our separate ways. But there wasn't anyone else involved for either of us until you and - and this woman he finally went away with Philip. And if I had agreed to divorce him he would be alive now.'

'No Jean. You mustn't think of it like that. He could have walked across a road and been run over, had an accident in the car, a heart attack, there are dozens of things that could have happened even if he hadn't been on that train at that time.'

They resumed their journey, and before they reached home Philip telephoned his wife again to say he wouldn't be able to get back that night. When he returned from the telephone booth Jean said, 'Well?'

'O.K. There won't be a search party out for me. So let's stop at the next reasonable looking pub or hotel, shall we?'

They had both brought an overnight bag, 'it's possible we won't be able to get back the same day. It is nearly three hundred miles after all', Philip had said last night.

51

They found a small hotel near Windsor and booked in for the night.

'Do you think that police officer thought it odd that Robert had a brand new suitcase Philip?'

'May have done. You handled it well darling. And that part of it was really none of his business. Once you'd identified the case and contents anyway.'

'Poor Robert.'

'Hey, come here.' He put his arms round her. 'I love you. You do know that, don't you? And somehow we're going to be together Jean, and soon. But if I leave without a divorce it means waiting a long time until we can legally marry.'

'I know.'

'And I'd need to stay near my job. I couldn't up sticks and go off as Robert appeared to be doing.'

'I know that too. I think that's one of the reasons I fell in love with you Philip. You're so logical. Unpredictability worries me and then I get angry.'

He released her slowly, and picked up the bedside telephone. 'I'll ask for an early call,' he said, 'then I can drop you before I go to work.'

She was smiling as she climbed into bed.

Chapter 5

Daisy had been at the dancing school for two weeks when Julien asked her for a date. He waited outside after collecting Alison on Friday afternoon, and rather shyly came forward.

'I - didn't like to speak to you in there, with everyone watching, but will you come out with me one evening?

She hesitated for a moment and he said, in a much firmer voice, 'We could have a meal, or go to the cinema or theatre, whatever you fancied.'

His dark eyes were smiling down at her and she heard herself say, 'I'd be happy to come.'

Alison tugged at his hand, 'Come on,' she said, 'we're missing the tele.'

'Tomorrow night all right? I'll call for you - what's your address?'

She was reluctant to have him come to the house, and finally they agreed to meet by the Leisure Centre.

'I'll have the car - it would be very easy to pick you up,' he said.

'No really. I'll - I'll look forward to it. Goodbye Julien. 'bye Alison,' she touched the child's fair head. 'See you on Monday.'

There was no surgery on Saturday evening, but the morning emergency one proved extra busy. A toddler who had swallowed a button, a couple of kitchen knife wounds - 'it's incredible how careless people are with household knives,' Ian said when the second one had

53

been dealt with; an elderly man with a bad attack of bronchitis and a young girl with earache.

They finished soon after twelve, and Ian suggested lunch out for the three of them. Sarah was off with Debbie for the day.

'You helped her a great deal when you accepted that temporary job at the ballet school, Daisy,' Jill said, 'I fancy she's a bit better tempered these days too, so maybe she's finally coming out of her rude stage.'

'How are you enjoying the job?' Ian chipped in. 'Has anything else fallen into place yet?'

'No, not exactly, but I'm convinced I did something in that line before because it is so familiar. I know what Pam is talking about - all the technical terms and everything. The job's helped me tremendously too. Given me more confidence. In fact I am actually going out with someone this evening. The father of one of the little girls in the preschool class.'

Jill and Ian looked up simultaneously.

'I - I think he's a widower. He's very young.'

'Good for you. Enjoy yourself,' Jill smiled at her. 'What did you say his name was?'

'I didn't, but its Julien. Julien Uppark.'

Julien was already there when she arrived at the venue that evening. A smile appeared on his rather serious looking face and Daisy realised that with her prevarication yesterday he had probably wondered if she would turn up.

She had thought the situation over pretty well since accepting the date and decided to continue the myth that she was a widow and had come to Torquay to be closer to her friends whom she now worked for as a receptionist.

During the evening Julien was bound to ask her about herself and she needed to be prepared. She felt nervous, but his diffidence helped her to be bolder in her approach.

They decided to eat first, and take a chance on a seat at the theatre in Babbacombe if they were both of a mind to go.

We don't want to have to rush a meal, do we?' Julien said, 'and sometimes it's simply good to talk. Maybe walk the food off along the shore later.'

'What about Alison. Will you have to be back at a special time because of babysitters?' she asked.

'Good heavens, no. Her mother will look after her tonight.' Seeing her startled look he added, 'I only collect her from dancing class because Anne is working until five each day and while I'm on my present job I'm free to do so.'

Daisy's heart sank. What *had* she done? Was his wife at home with her child - or children, while Julien...

'Anne?' The surprise in her voice echoed the question.

'My sister. Mum and dad have a large house and Anne and her husband Tom have the basement flat. I live with mum and dad when I'm working here, but take lodgings when I'm away.'

Daisy couldn't understand the relief that flowed through her veins when he said that. After all, would it have mattered so much if he was married and Alison was his child as she had thought. After tonight she probably wouldn't see him again, except when he shot into the school to collect Alison. But she knew it *did* matter that she saw him again and she told herself sternly to behave.

They went to a quiet licenced restaurant, where the white tablecloths were reflected in the sparkling glasses, and an unobtrusive but very smartly dressed waiter ushered them over the crimson carpet to a corner table.

It was the beginning of a wonderful summer. There were so many meeting points, and she was surprised how easily she could chat with Julien. For one thing he didn't fire questions at her, and although he couldn't know how grateful she was for this, she realised suddenly that she probably wasn't the sort of person who liked a barrage of questions anyway. He did ask when she had come to live in Torquay and she told him, 'after my husband died, and it wasn't so long ago so I'd really rather not talk about it.'

'Of course.' He looked embarrassed for a moment, then he said, 'You and me both - oh I wasn't married, but my fiancé died last year. We would have married this spring - it was all planned. She was involved in a three car pileup on her way to work one icy morning...'

Instinctively she reached out, and his hand met hers across the table. After that they talked of Torquay, of ballet, which he laughingly said embarrassed him. 'All those little girls in their standout skirts, I feel a proper twit walking in there for Alison, and she always sits at the end so I have to go the length of that corridor.'

Because she didn't know the area they visited all the tourist spots, but she loved Babbacombe best. Walking along the clifftop and looking down into the wonderful bay she became exhilarated. There was no familiarity about it, no sense of having been before, simply a freedom of spirit.

At first she *did* look for signs of things she may have known, maybe from holidays, but after a while, when she was with Julien all her attention was focused on him and she really did forget.

She was working Saturday mornings, but from after lunch, and often all day on Sunday, she and Julien explored. They went to Brixham, and Dartmouth, Buckfast Abbey - nearer home to Cockington and Paignton, they wandered around little country churches, Sunday markets, went for long walks, which both of them enjoyed, often finishing at a rustic pub for lunch. Saturday evenings were spent together, and it was on such a Saturday evening that Julien introduced her to his family.

His mum and dad, Anne and her husband Tom, and the pet dog and cat.

She felt welcomed as soon as she rather shyly entered the room with Julien. It had taken all her courage to go - twice she had made excuses, and she knew she was making a drama out of what should have been a natural process.

'I'm not really very good when I first meet people Julien, it's different now with you, but I get a bit tongue-tied with strangers.'

'Not to worry Daisy. They're not a bit stiff, and they are longing to meet you. I keep telling them how gorgeous you are,' he added, laughing.

'That makes me even more nervous. I know it's silly, but I - I can't help it.'

'I'll be there, and we needn't stay all evening. Just pop in for an hour, then take ourselves off somewhere.' His quiet voice gave her confidence, and when his smiling sister Anne said as she greeted her, 'At last I can size up my opposition. Alison never stops talking about you Daisy. It's "My dancing teacher, Mrs. Shore has pretty hair. My dancing teacher Mrs. Shore is ever so dainty." Oh and the latest one - when I grumbled at her the other day, "My dancing teacher *never* shouts at me like that."'

Amid the laughter she found herself propelled into the room and within minutes she was joining in as though she had always known the entire family. Anne was noisier than Julien, but she had the same high cheekbones which gave her an intellectual appearance - in her case instantly belayed by her vivacious fooling around. Conversation flowed easily - there were no personal history's bandied about - Daisy was taken over the Victorian house to see how well it had lent itself to conversion into two flats when Anne, Tom and Alison had come to live there a few years ago.

The original hour stretched into three, and when he took her back to Murray House Julien said quietly, 'You see, it wasn't so bad, was it? None of them are ogres.'

'*Julien*.'

Sometimes she thought it strange that her amnesia seldom interfered when she was with him. Conversation was usually about an incident that had happened to them - an event at the ballet school, or a funny thing at Julien's work, and the past didn't intrude. The present became increasingly important for both of them and she knew her happiness showed.

Once or twice they visited the cabaret at local hotels, and several times they went dancing. He was a quiet, but very good dancer. His height and general bearing, (away from the ballet classes when he tried to look as though he wasn't there) were in his favour - tall, graceful, and very light on his feet. Daisy followed easily, and laughed delightedly when he expressed concern that she, with her 'expertise', might find him clumsy.

'You're actually better than I am,' she said, 'you really do glide over the floor, and Julien, it's heaven to dance with you.'

In his job as an electronics engineer for a large company he travelled around the British Isles, often spending several months based in different areas, and this project in the south-west was scheduled for a few more months, he told her.

The thing that bothered her most as the summer progressed was the knowledge that she had been untruthful with him. How *could* I have known on that first date that I'd eventually feel like this, she asked herself in the privacy of her bedroom at Murray House.

She wished with all her heart that she had had the courage to tell him she couldn't remember anything before that terrible moment in hospital when the Sister asked her name. The blackness that descended when she tried to recall 'before' still made her tremble with nervousness. No-one who hasn't experienced a loss of memory can have any conception of the panic, she thought. Since her story of widowhood, which she never enlarged on to anyone, she had more confidence, she wasn't a blank with no memory reserves to draw on, at least not to the people she was with.

She said to Jill one day, 'I don't believe people value their memories enough. The ordinary little things of everyday - the people you know, the ideas you have - these are part of you and when they aren't there, there's a great void which puts you at the bottom of a dark pit without footholds.'

Jill reached over and held both her hands. 'But you are coming out of that pit Daisy - you are, even now, building memories. Memories which, with what are still there behind this curtain as Ian calls it, will be your footholds. One day the clouds will shift and you'll remember, I know you will.'

July and August found Torquay packed with holidaymakers, in spite of the not so summery weather, and Daisy sometimes sat on the promenade after morning surgery and scanned the faces of the people walking by. Was there someone there who belonged to her - or who had once been connected with her? Was there someone who came to search for her even as she was looking for them? Because, whatever Ian and Jill, and Dr Plymouth said to try to cheer her, there *had* to be a

60

reason for her being on that train to Torquay. Was she visiting someone here? If so, why hadn't they come forward? She felt pretty sure she hadn't lived here because nothing about it was familiar to her, not as the ballet school was, and since her friendship with Julien she had seen quite a lot of it. When her thoughts became too entangled she made herself stop and concentrate on something else, but nothing could alter the fact that she had deceived Julien and the longer it went on the worse it would become.

It was the end of August when Julien asked her to marry him. 'I know it's early days for you Daisy, and I do understand how it is, believe me I do, but I have a reason for asking you now instead of waiting a while longer. You see I've a chance of a good job in London.'

'Oh Julien. Julien. I - I don't think I could marry anyone.'

'I half expected you to say that,' he countered, 'but if I take this job - and I'd be a fool not to Daisy, will you think about what I've said. I could come and see you at weekends until you - well until you've made up your mind. I do love you so Daisy. I've not said anything before because I - well I thought it was too soon, but you must have realised how it was - how I felt. Is there some hope Daisy? For later, maybe. I promise I won't rush you?

'Julien, please *stop* - there's something I have to tell you. Something I should have said a long while ago.'

He kept his arm round her. 'I'm listening,'

She didn't know where to begin, and after a moment or two he tried to help. 'I suppose you're not a widow,

61

only separated and your husband won't divorce you. Is that the problem darling?' He held her hand tighter, and his voice was gentle.

'If it were only that Julien.'

'Well?' He rested his face against her hair; his hand still comfortingly clasping hers.

'I didn't tell you the whole truth when we first met, Julien. I'm - not *sure* if I am a widow', the words rushed out now, 'you see I can't remember,' nervously she rubbed one thumb against the wedding ring, 'but I was wearing this when I was found and so - so I have to presume that I am.'

'You mean - you can't remember anything?'

Close to tears now she nodded.

'But - forgive me darling, but, but how did it happen, your loss of memory?'

She fought off the tears. Whatever the outcome it was a relief that Julien knew. 'A train crash. In the spring, you probably remember. The London train crashed not far out of the town. I don't even know if I boarded it in London - but I think I did because the only unclaimed handbag had a single ticket to Torquay in it.'

'And your name I suppose. And presumably an address?'

She shook her head. 'No Julien. There was nothing, absolutely nothing in that bag to identify its owner. A - a handkerchief with some daisies on - that's why they called me Daisy, the single ticket, and a - an elderly purse with three hundred pounds in , so you see I can't m-marry anyone Julien,' she was crying now, the tears raining unheeded down her cheeks, 'because somewhere I may have a husband, and...'

'Darling.' His strong arms were around her, his body muffling her sobs. 'My darling Daisy, it doesn't *matter* who you are, I love you and I want to marry you. You love me, don't you?' Gently he eased her from him so he could look into her face. 'Oh it complicates things I suppose, but together we can sort it out. If you are a widow, there's no problem, and if you're not then we have to - to search for your husband. You could have been running away from him - I mean, with that amount of money in your bag and a single ticket, it sounds as if you didn't mean to return...'

'What do you think I've *been* doing. I've thought and thought until I've felt I should go mad, but there's nothing in my mind before I woke up in hospital. Oh they told me I was found wandering along the embankment - that made their task more difficult because they don't even know which carriage I was in.'

'The newspapers. They'll run a story to find out who you are...'

'No Julien, *no*. I won't do that. It's a horrible idea and I couldn't bear to have reporters questioning and guessing, and probing.'

'But surely you want to find out who you are?'

'Of course I do.' Her brown eyes sparked at him, 'but not *that* way. I shall remember myself one day - all the doctors are convinced of it.'

'Are you?'

63

'Ye - No, not really. When you struggle to remember every waking hour as I have done and there's still this great void, it's hard to believe they are right. Sometimes I am almost certain they are, you know when little things fall into place, then, no matter how I try, there's nothing there and I lose faith again.'

His arms came round her, 'You haven't answered my important question darling. Do you love me and will you marry me?'

'But how...'

'We'll do our own detective work. Quietly if that's the way you want it. If you are still married we'll sort it out somehow. That train crash was in the spring you said - well I was working away then, but I do recall them talking about it at home.'

'Dr Plymouth, at the hospital, and of course Ian and Jill, kept it quiet that I was suffering from amnesia - you see they thought my memory would have returned by now. Oh, Ian doesn't say so, but I know he never expected it to take all this time, and now - oh Julien, what are we going to do?'

Chapter 6

Julien's new job was due to begin in the middle of September. 'Come with me, darling,' he pleaded. 'We can live quietly, *separately* - I'm not asking you to do anything so terrible, am I? If we can find rooms - a couple of bedsits in the same house - just think how marvellous it would be. And we can pursue our own line of investigation as to how you came to be on that train - it will surely be easier from London than from here?

She thought about it well before she agreed. She loved him and in the short while since they had met, knew she had come alive again. She still desperately wanted to regain her memory, *but*, if she never did, she could go wholeheartedly into a new life with Julien by her side. He at least *knew* he was free of encumbrances.

'The important thing is that we love each other,' he said one evening when they were standing on the seafront romantically watching the moon over the water. 'With that going for us we can tackle anything.'

'What if we have children, Julien?'

'I don't understand. Eventually I think it would be great, but it's something in the future. Right now I'm more concerned with the present.'

'But - I might have a disease - something they could inherit. With no knowledge of what has gone before, how do I know?'

'Daisy, oh my dearest, don't let's meet these problems before we need. You look healthy enough to me, and there are such facilities as check-ups, especially when

65

someone is pregnant. Believe me I know because I was dodging around the place when Anne had Alison. As I see it there's only one issue. Do you love me?'

His dark eyes gazed into hers. 'Daisy?' His voice was soft, caressing, and for a moment there was a glimmer of - what? That tantalising feeling of having been here before. Was it the voice or the words.

'Well?' His face was close to hers, and she saw the love in his eyes, heard it in his tone.

'Yes, Julien. I - I love you. I don't know if I have any right to, but I do.'

'Then that's all that matters. Oh, we won't give up trying to find out who you are, but to me you'll always be Daisy, beloved Daisy, no matter what. I just want to be with you and look after you now for the rest of my life.'

'But we'll have to find out before I can marry you, darling. It wouldn't be legal otherwise.'

'We will. We'll trace your past together, and we'll sort it out together, and then, for the rest of our lives it will be you and me. Daisy I love you so...' their lips met in a lingering kiss while the moonlight chased the gentle ripple of the waves as they broke on the shore.

When she told Ian and Jill what she was planning to do Jill said quickly, 'That's great news Daisy, but... oh dear this is going to sound awful because I know in my heart you'll be happy together, but you haven't known him long and...' she bit her lower lip, 'why don't you give it a few more months?' The last sentence came out in a rush and Daisy gazed at her friend.

'You think our feelings for each other will change?'

Jill shook her head. 'No, I don't. But I *am* afraid for you rushing into a marriage. I can't see the need. If you love each other why not wait a while and... and when your amnesia is cured you can go forward easily.'

Close to tears at her friend's seeming criticism Daisy turned away, and quickly Jill came over to sit on the arm of her chair, her hand resting gently on Daisy's shoulder.

'I'm only concerned for you dear - I don't want you to have more complications.'

Ian, who until now had been silent, said, 'Julien's a fine man. I like him and one only has to see the two of you together to feel the empathy between you. But be sure it's love Daisy, and not a sort of groping for a background. In any case you won't be able to marry until it's proved that you haven't a husband alive somewhere.'

Daisy covered her face with both hands and her words came out like a muffled echo. 'I thought you'd both be glad for me - there's enough obstacles surrounding me already. Julien has strength and a clear mind and he loves me. We shall try to unravel my past because we want to be married properly and we can't without knowing.' Nervously she twisted the ring on her finger. It was looser now than it had been, and as she gazed at it a shaft of sunlight through the window caught it, and seemed to turn it into a ball of sparking gold. Surely, surely you would recall the day someone you loved placed a ring on your finger. Surely you would have *some* recollection in your mind of a service, of an exchange of vows, of promises to someone... but there was nothing there, only this thick grey blanket of sludge. She changed her position

67

to escape the sun now shining into her eyes and catching the tears glinting there, and Ian said quietly, 'When were you thinking of going to London Daisy?'

'Not immediately. I won't go until you've found a new receptionist. I owe you that.'

'You owe us nothing Daisy. You've worked hard and the patients will miss you I know, to say nothing of Jill and I - and Sarah,' he added. 'And there's always a home for you here - remember that, won't you?'

She escaped to her room and throwing herself on the bed, sobbed uncontrollably. If she quarrelled with Jill and Ian she would break the only contacts she could remember...

'Daisy, can I come with you?' Sarah's eyes were bright with excitement. If I was with you mum and dad would let me go I'm sure. They trust you but not me,' she added petulantly. 'I'd be no bother, honestly, and I'd love to live and work in London.'

'You haven't finished college.'

'That doesn't matter. I'm of an age to leave, and I'm only there for want of something better to do. Now in London...'

'No. I can't take you with me. I'm sorry Sarah,' Daisy said more gently now, 'but you should finish college and get some qualifications. You know that as well as I do, and you're a brilliant artist - it would be utterly stupid not to finish the course.'

'But it's so boring. And if I were in London I could get work, fill in somewhere, I wouldn't care what I did -

waitressing, bar work, pavement artist...' she giggled. 'I can imagine mum if she came to town and I was drawing on the pavement, can't you?'

'Seriously darling, much as I'd love to have you with me, I'll not agree. But you can always visit. Come straight from college on a Friday for the weekend.'

Sarah pouted. 'That won't be the same as living in town. Gosh, I'll be glad when I'm out working and earning so I can please myself more. This town won't see much of me, I'll tell you.' She flounced out.

Pam from the dancing school was disappointed too. She had kept Daisy on even after her original assistant returned. 'The school's expanding, and you're a born teacher,' she said.

Was she? Had she been a ballet teacher before. Her life now seemed to be divided into before and after. And if she was a teacher it seemed likely to be in London, or the provinces, for she never had the feeling of living in Torquay before the crash. Or she could have been a dancer herself, in which case once up there she could quietly check that theory out.

What still bothered her tremendously was the fact that no-one had come forward to enquire about her. If she had family and friends, it seemed logical that someone would know she was on that train and try to find out what happened to her. Or at least, after all this time, wonder why they hadn't heard and do a bit of detective work around Torquay. Unless, as Julien said, she was running away from her husband, and he had decided not to come after her. 'That would also explain why no-one else has bothered,' he said one night, 'because it certainly wouldn't be prudent to interfere between husband and wife.'

A lot of things still worried her. The fact that she had no identification whatsoever on her person, and all that money.

'You obviously drew it out and decided to begin a new life,' was Julien's verdict, 'and I believe you were travelling alone.' She had told him how the police took her to see the victims who were killed. 'I recognised no-one Julien, no-one. But that doesn't mean some of them didn't belong to me, does it?'

'And the injured too, none of them said there was anyone else travelling with them.'

'There is still one way to encourage people to come forward, if you could only bring yourself to do it.'

'You mean the newspapers? I've already told you I couldn't. Everyone would stare, who knows what sort of crazy letters I'd get...'

'O.K. O.K. But everyone *wouldn't* know. One picture in the national papers - you needn't even tell them the full story. I mean about the money - simply your total lack of remembrance, and that you had no identification papers on you.'

'They'd find out. Sometimes even now I feel that everyone I meet must know. So how much worse it would be if they really did.'

'Nonsense, it would...'

'NO, NO, NO. If you don't think you can cope with life with me as I am, then we'd better part now.'

70

'It isn't me who can't cope Daisy, it's you who want to find out about your background, and who are refusing to listen to alternative methods. That's O.K by me,' his voice softened, 'and maybe you're right and the publicity would be too much. But if you really want to find out who you are, I'd be surprised if the media didn't bring results.'

'I won't do it.' She swallowed a sob. 'I wo- I *can't* do it, Julien.'

She thought he would take her in his arms, tell her it didn't matter, one day she'd remember, and meanwhile he would always be there. Instead he patted her hand and said, 'As it's such anathema to you I won't mention that method again. Only you can decide if you want to come, and it was wrong of me to try to persuade you.' He turned away.

'*Julien*.' In that moment she knew she had to heal the breach. She couldn't let him go to London with this quarrel between them, and she wanted more than anything else to be with Julien forever. What had gone before was obviously over, and Julien was here, loving her as she loved him.

'Julien,' she said again, 'don't let us fight. Not over this anyway. I will come to London. I always want to be near you. I'll try to find my true identity, but I can't do it that way. I don't know why, only that it makes me go cold with fear. Whether that's something in my background, or in my nature I'm not sure. I know I'm being stubborn, irrationally so it probably seems, over that issue, but that's me, Julien. That's the only me I know...'

71

'Darling, it's the one I love - the one I hope will stay with me always.'

Sarah came to her room later that night when she heard her go in.

'Just to say I'm sorry if I sounded like a spoilt child earlier Daisy. I didn't mean to add to your problems. And I will come up sometimes if the offer still stands.'

'Of course it does. It will be something for me to look forward to as well, because I shall have to start all over again, without the support of the friends I've made here. It's quite a daunting prospect Sarah, and I am quaking a bit.'

'You've got us. I mean if it goes wrong. But you and Julien make a great couple. I don't know why you're fussing about looking into your past, apart from naturally wanting to know, but from the point of view of being able to marry, well, why don't you just live together? That's what I'd do?'

Daisy smiled into Sarah's unusually serious face. 'I know. But I've still got to find out about *me*.'

As the girl turned to go Daisy said, 'Sarah. Thanks. Julien and I actually quarrelled about it tonight. Oh we've sorted it out now, and it's going to be all right.'

Julien began his new job towards the end of September. He found a room in a lodging house, 'Its' quite large,' he told her, 'bed that pushes into the wall and a couple of armchairs. Over by the window there's a table and couple of chairs, and the other end of the room's the kitchen area, sink, cooker, small fridge - it'll do well enough until

72

you come up and hopefully then we can find something together.'

They had decided that she would follow him to London in October. That way she could train someone to take over her job in the surgery, and he would look around for another flat or bedsit, and a job, for her.

The night before he left they went for a meal to the restaurant he had taken her to on their first date.

The same elderly but elegant waiter took them to their table, and as he pulled her chair out for her she felt tears pricking her eyes.

'All right darling,' Julien gazed across at her lovingly.

'Mmm. Just being stupid really, but it's such a happy memory - the first night we went out together. I suppose it's that really - I've years of memories to catch up with.'

'The bonus for me is that I'll be in all of them sweetheart.' He reached across and held her hand, and as he stroked her fingers he said, 'How about an engagement ring my love. At least you could wear my ring while we're waiting to find out if you're free to marry me. And you haven't one with a gem in - only that wedding ring. I'm not leaving until tomorrow afternoon - can you meet me in the morning and we'll get one?'

She chose a pretty diamond cluster – 'Why don't you have something bigger than that,' Julien said.

'I love that one - do you like it too?'

He smiled at her, 'Of course I do. It suits your small fingers. And it will do until I put my own plain gold band on.'

She kept looking at it after he had left for London. What if a husband turned up after she had married Julien. No, no, of course not. That wouldn't be possible because she wouldn't be allowed to get married until it was certain she was free to do so. That was the awful part of this amnesia. Surely when this happened to people there were usually others in their lives who could tell them about the past. Others who had been part of that other life before the darkness. For her there was nothing - nothing at all remembered from before the crash. She couldn't even recall the accident itself or walking along the embankment which, according to the ambulance men is where she was found. It was as though life began in that hospital ward with the frightening knowledge that she hadn't any idea who she was. Nor had anyone else. The loneliness of her situation hit her afresh after Julien left, and when, a week before she was due to join him she told Maude she was moving to London, she wasn't prepared for the scene it caused.

'London. What will you do in London?'

She hadn't mentioned Julien's new job, and she answered quietly, 'Look for work, build a new life for myself.'

'But why London? Why not stay here. You've a job here, two in fact, and if you wanted to you could break away and run your own school I daresay. If not here, then a bit further along the coast.'

'I know Maude, but I have my reasons. I'll miss Torquay, I've grown to love it this summer, but I'll return sometimes, visit friends...' to her dismay she started to cry.

'Hey come on luv, what's up? You can tell me you know.' But all she could do was turn away and sob. Maude reached over and cuddled her, 'Happen you'll feel better if you talk about it,' she said, 'whatever it is, and I may be a nosy old woman, but I've never given a secret away yet, so it'll be safe with me.' She passed her a handkerchief, 'Here, dry your eyes and I'll make us a cup of tea.'

Five minutes later as she walked into the tiny sitting room Maude caught her breath, almost dropped the tray she was carrying and said, *I've got it*. Ever since I've known you I've wondered where I've seen you before. You were on that train that crashed in the spring. I remember now. Oh, my dear, is that how your husband died?'

Daisy stared at her friend - and knew the time had come when she had to be honest. Admit to those who she now realised cared about her, that she wasn't a widow, at least not as far as she knew...

'No, Maude. I've not been absolutely straight with you these last months. Not just you, not with anyone, but there is a reason. I simply can't remember anything.'

Maude's grey eyes seemed to enlarge as she gazed back at Daisy. 'You - can't remember. What - not anything at all?'

Miserably Daisy nodded. 'I've tried,' she said brokenly, 'God knows I've tried until my brain seemed like bursting, but there's nothing. It's as though I first existed when I woke up in that hospital bed.'

'But the doctors, they - surely they can do something?'

'Apparently not. It's a question of time. At least that's what they keep telling me,' she finished with a bitter tone in her voice. 'I'm beginning not to believe them anymore.'

Still looking bemused Maude passed her the cup of tea. 'Here, drink it before it goes cold, luv. You've quite stunned me - honest you have. If only I'd realised; I must have hurt you quite a bit with some of my prying, Daisy. I know I do fire questions at folk sometimes when I'm interested in 'em, but I'd never want to hurt you dear. Oh my goodness, I don't know what to think.'

Daisy sipped her tea. It was good that Maudie knew the truth now. Suddenly she realised how she hated lying to people who had become her friends. She really did feel lighter hearted now she had come into the open again. Yet she couldn't do it in a general way. She knew she could not do as Julien had suggested and let the newspapers get hold of the story and advertise for anyone who knew her, but among those she had grown fond of this summer in Torquay she could only feel relief that at last they knew the truth.

They were onto their second cup of tea before Daisy realised the implications of Maudie's sudden remembrance of where she had seen her before.

'Maudie.' She couldn't keep the excitement from her voice, even in uttering that one word. 'Maudie, how did you know I was on that train? Where did you see me that

76

day – and, and.' She put her cup carefully back into the saucer because her hand was trembling so, 'did I have anyone with me?'

'I had been staying with a friend in London for a few days,' Maudie said, 'but I only came back as far as Newton Abbot because I'd promised to visit a friend there too. When I heard about the crash I was in a cold sweat I can tell you. Betty, that's my pal in Newton Abbot, was too. 'Its fate,' she said to me, 'that's what it is, fate that we planned this, otherwise you would have been on that train through to Torquay.'

'But you – you remembered me. Remembered seeing me, Maudie. Try, oh please try to recall exactly. Did you speak to me for instance? And was I alone?'

'No, you weren't alone. There was a gentleman with you. I remember now. I first noticed you when I walked through to the buffet.'

She stopped and Daisy said, 'Well go on. What happened? I mean, to make you notice me?'

Maudie rose and walked over to her chair. Balancing on the arm she put her hands on Daisy's shoulders. Then, swallowing hard she said, 'I noticed you because you looked so together, so right, so in love I suppose. Reminded me of my Jack, how we used to be, and I envied you for a minute.   You were still talking and listening and looking at each other in that – that special way when I came back with my cuppa. Then,' convulsively she gripped Daisy's shoulders, 'just before we reached Newton Abbot I thought I'd go to the loo and I walked

77

through. The one at the end of my carriage was engaged and so I carried on, and I saw you again.'

'Yes.'

'Well that's it. Oh no, when I came out you were alone. The young man had gone.'

'But can't you remember anything else? I mean, what was he like Maudie, this, this man I was travelling with?'

But Maudie didn't know and was clearly embarrassed now at having said so much. 'You know me Daisy, shoot my mouth off when I shouldn't. Maybe I misinterpreted your looks. Maybe he was someone sitting next to you and you were passing the time of day with each other.'

'No.' Daisy was shouting now, 'of course we weren't. We couldn't have been. You said yourself that we looked as though we were in love. So who was he, Maudie? Was he my husband, and if so where is he now? Whoever he is why doesn't he come forward? That is if he knew me, if we were together?'

She told Ian and Jill that evening. Half of her wanted to keep this new knowledge to herself until she had absorbed it, thought about it, and maybe even remembered who the man was. The practical, realistic side of her knew she wouldn't recall the past simply because a sudden look had jogged Maudie's memory. If only it were that easy. If anything it complicated things. She was just beginning to accept that because no-one had come forward to enquire about her she was footloose and fancy free and could team up with Julien. Now she knew she would need to stay here a while longer and try to sort it out.

Ian was pleased with the revelations. 'It seemed as though we were all facing a blank wall, Daisy,' he said, 'now we do know you were travelling with someone, and as they haven't come forward then it would be reasonable to suppose that it was one of the two unidentified people from the crash.'

She lowered her gaze from the gleam of excitement in his eyes, and he said gently, 'Would you like me to deal with it initially? See the police and Maudie, and try to piece a little more of the puzzle together?'

'Yes please Ian. Is that cowardly of me? I suppose it is I – '

'Not at all. In any case it will be easier for me to probe and question than for you to do so. The police will probably want to talk to you again. But after that I think you should go ahead with your plans to go to London with Julien. A complete change might be a good thing you know, and when you feel ready, you could return to the ticket office, at the time you must have done on that day, and in acting out what probably happened, buying a ticket, walking to the platform, well sometimes something gels. I'm not saying it will, only maybe. And only when you feel able to cope with what you may remember, because if it was your husband or someone you loved who died in that crash Daisy, your grief will start from the time of remembering.'

She was amazed at how difficult it was to leave Torquay. Pam from the dancing school, all the children, even the original assistant who was now back, seemed genuinely sorry she was going. Of them all Pam was the only one who knew about her amnesia, and she asked Daisy about it a couple of days before she left.

'I'm being very inquisitive I know, but I've grown so fond of you Daisy, and you're such a great dancer that I'm sure that's what you did before the accident. Look how you always know what I'm talking about without me ever having to explain. I've watched you when you are demonstrating a step to the children. You have been trained as a dancer Daisy, I'd stake my reputation on it.'

'I think you're probably right, Pam. When I've settled myself in London I'll try the ballet schools and see if anyone remembers me, or if I recall any of them. I'm at home when I'm dancing and I agree with you that my knowledge is more than a natural aptitude for the art. I too think that I must have had training at some stage, but, well until now I've not felt ready to tackle the question and all it entails. But there comes a time when you can no longer put off something as important as this.'

'Do please keep in touch, and if you come this way again to live, there will be a job here for you.' Daisy escaped before the tears came. She wondered if she had always been a person who cried easily, or if it was because so many people were kind to her, and in spite of her reticent nature where that personal life of hers was concerned, she desperately needed these friends.

She left Torquay quietly, refusing to allow anyone to see her off. 'No, Jill, please don't be offended, but I simply couldn't face it. I'll have a taxi and I will let you know when I arrive, I promise.'

She didn't tell Maudie the day or time of her departure. 'In a few days,' was as near as she would go, 'but I'll write as soon as I can, and I'll be back some day.'

It was a clear, cold morning and she climbed into the taxi knowing she was now on her own. These dear friends, the only ones she had, must be left behind while she delved into the past she couldn't remember, but which was so important now that she and Julien had acknowledged their feelings for each other.

On the train she tried unsuccessfully to think of other things than the crash that had started this for her. She wasn't nervous that the same thing might happen again, for she didn't recall the moments beforehand, they were wiped out with the rest. Yet, she thought, I might have instinctively felt the terror of another train journey, but I don't.

She even smiled to herself as she recalled the studied carefulness Ian and Jill had practised this last few days when her intended trip was mentioned. Bless them, how I shall miss everyone. Resolutely she took her book from the pocket of the small travel bag she bought last week, and forced herself to concentrate on the printed words.

'But darling that's marvellous. Our first lead.' Julien kissed her. 'Now you're up here with me we can follow it up. You'll never be alone again, I promise you. We'll go round the ballet companies together, and if you don't want to ask the questions yourself I'll –'

'Don't pamper me, Julien, and don't treat me like a child. You can't feel pain over someone you don't know –

81

not in the same way as – as someone you really are in love with. I've got to find out who he was, this man Maudie thought I was travelling with. I'm sure now, in my mind, that I was with him. She was certain you see, until she realised the implications, then she backed off a bit and said it was only conjecture.'

'You said there were two unidentified people, Daisy. What happened about them?'

'The police advertised I believe. You see I didn't want to know and I never told them I couldn't remember. Strictly speaking I suppose Doctor Plymouth at the hospital should have told them, but he felt it might hamper my recovery, because I was in a bit of a state about it all you know.'

'Naturally.' He walked over to a sideboard and took out two wine glasses. 'Here, I bought us a bottle to celebrate the start of our life together.' He was struggling with the corkscrew, and added laughing, 'One of the first items I'll buy is a decent bottle opener, 'the one that's here is diabolical.' The cork came with a resounding pop, and Julien quickly poured two glasses of red wine and handed her one.

'To us,' he said, clinking his glass against hers, 'and our future.'

'Our future.' She echoed his words, then her hand holding the glass began to tremble and the tremble became an earthquake that travelled up her arm, then all over her body, and her glass crashed to the floor, the crimson liquid splashing over the dull grey carpet and staining it with brilliant colour.'

82

'It's all right, it was an accident and there's no damage done. Please stop crying darling.' Julien cradled her in his arms, trying to stop the flood of tears that suddenly gushed forth and which she could not control.

'I'm so sorry,' she whispered a little while later as they both tried to scrub the wine stain from the carpet, 'I simply don't know what came over me.'

Julien, who thought her memory might have returned when they were toasting each other, tried not to sound disappointed. 'There, think it's all off. And there's plenty more in the bottle. Let's try again.'

Later still when she had gone to her own room on the floor below, she relived in her mind, the moments when she had begun to tremble so. There had been *something*, some fragment of memory that haunted her tantalisingly. It was there in that moment, yet when she tried to recall it, it had gone.

The house Julien and Daisy now called home was a four storied Victorian villa, long since divided into one and two room flatlets. Hers had a largish living room, with a divider for the kitchen area. The bedroom was small, had probably once been a sizable bathroom, but it was adequate for her needs. The bathroom and toilet, one on each floor, were at the end of the hallway, near the stairs. Fully furnished, including crockery, cutlery and linen she was grateful to have a place of her own that was yet so close to Julien's. His flat, at the end near the bathroom on the floor above, was similar, but the living room was a

83

fraction smaller. The great thing was that it was close to his present work, and that they were together.

She fell asleep that first evening in London, glad that she had made the decision now to unravel whatever was in that past she must have experienced before. And grateful that Julien looked like being in her future.

Chapter 7

Jean was worried. I can't be pregnant, she thought, surely not. Yet all the signs were there. The missed period, the morning sickness. This last week she had dragged herself to the office feeling terrible. One morning when it had gone on longer than usual she was late for the first time in her career. Everyone was kind to her, and at least they didn't comment on her appearance - probably attributed it to grief, she thought.

She and Philip tried to meet for lunch twice a week, the arrangement had been in force for a long time, but the atmosphere wasn't conducive to confiding her fears to him. Although they varied the venue, there was always too much noise because they had to choose fast service, and most of the workforce of the city did too. By lunchtime she was usually feeling fit again anyway, and their need was simply that of seeing each other and making arrangements for being together...

So far since Robert's death Philip had not come to the house, and Jean leant across the table one Thursday toward the end of the month and said,

'Philip, do you think you could come along one evening after work.'

'I don't think that would be very wise my dear. It's too soon. We've both got jobs to think of; we don't want a scandal. In any case I've got plans so we can be together for always.'

'When?'

'What?'

'When can we be together for always - and how?'

'Well,' he laughed nervously, 'I'm not going to murder my wife or anything, but I'm working on her and I think she's wavering...'

'Oh my God. Philip,' someone pushed by her chair to reach their coat hanging on the rack behind, and she stopped.

'Listen darling, it's the photography club outing the first Sunday of next month, so we can spend the whole day together. Do whatever you want, go wherever you like...'

She tried to keep her composure. It was so unlike her to be panicky about anything, but his calmness, his business-like attitude which she normally admired made her want to scream. Everything and everybody made her want to scream this last few days. Gritting her teeth she whispered, 'I've got to see you urgently and properly. We can't talk like this, and Philip, oh Philip, we *have* to talk.'

'All right, I'll try. But we don't want to jeopardise our chances. If she puts a private detective onto me we'll have had it. I have to think of my job, for both our sakes. And I've told you she is definitely coming round to the idea of divorce - she knows it's all over with us and...'

'Excuse me.' Someone else after their coat. Jean stood up and pushed the chair away in frustrated anger.

'I saw more of you when Robert was alive than I do now he's dead. If we're finished, washed up, *then say so*. Don't make excuses to me Philip. I need to know where I stand.'

If she hadn't felt so uptight she would have laughed at the expression of utter amazement on his face then. 'But of course we're not washed up. I'm looking ahead to our future darling, I've told you...'

They were jostling for their own coats now, and his cheek brushed against hers, 'I do love you, you know I do. You're having a bad day, that's all. I'll 'phone you at home when I take the dog out this evening. I have to get back now, I'm on the counter this afternoon.'

Although Jean and Robert had met at one of his bank social evenings which she had attended with a girlfriend who had then also worked there, her job was with a firm of solicitors. It was a large practice, and although she was friendly enough with everyone who worked there, she had no real mate. 'Bit of a cold fish' had been the general opinion among most of the staff, 'but a good worker and not a gossip.' When she was widowed they all felt sorry, and each did what she could in her own way to include her in office interests and activities. She realised her sudden climb to near popularity was sparked off by compassion, and while she felt grateful to a certain extent she also felt very embarrassed.

Back home she made herself a pot of tea and scrambled some eggs. Her thoughts kept returning to the first time she was pregnant, so soon after marrying Robert. She hadn't especially wanted a baby then, but at least it was conceived within wedlock. You should have thought of the consequences my girl, she told herself. It's too late now. She had lost the other baby just when she was used to the idea of motherhood, but she quickly dismissed the thought this time. Of course it would mean giving up her job, which she enjoyed, and which brought in a good wage. She certainly didn't fancy moving downwards in the money stakes. Perhaps there would be something she could do from home once the child arrived. Working on her own would not bother her - in fact, she thought she would probably enjoy it.

Philip did ring her about nine o'clock. She was calm then, having sat down after her dinner and written out several lists of possibilities. The one she wanted most she *didn't* commit to paper; it stayed in her head and her heart - to marry Philip.

She knew people sometimes thought she was hard and standoffish, but she couldn't alter her nature. Perhaps that was what had drawn her to Robert in the first place - that he was so opposite, warm, caring, loving. Well she too was loving, but it didn't often show. Her passion for Philip was deep and strong, and they were two of a kind. His precision matched her own.

If only they had met before both were committed. When she first fell in love with him she had thought it was a lost cause. She and Robert, although still living in the same house, were poles apart, yet her conventional upbringing stopped her from looking at anyone else. When she met Philip at that bank social her world really *did* turn a somersault. For many months he was a dream in her heart, and when they met again one Saturday afternoon in the town and he told her she had featured in his dreams every night since, she began to hope. She recalled the many serious conversations they'd had since about their respective responsibilities, and she remembered too the nights she had lain in bed and wished with all her heart she could do what she knew many people would - what Robert eventually *had* done - leave.

Yet none of that counted now, because Robert was dead - the last thing she would have expected was to be a widow. She had wondered how she and Philip could conceivably come together, but *that* possibility hadn't crossed her mind. Robert was young and healthy... the sadness in her was for their youth, for the waste of a life. It had given her freedom, but it had left a huge ache in her heart.

Her immediate problem had to be this baby. She knew the Jean beneath the surface - the Jean who loved Philip, was the real one. The one who took chances, the one who loved deeply and regardlessly; but the other, more conventional Jean could not be denied. The conventional Jean was the one who was uppermost, but the buried Jean was the one who was the strongest in feeling. Fleetingly she wondered if she would have felt differently had that first baby lived. One day she would tell Philip about that, because she wanted their relationship to always be open and true. She wanted him eventually to know everything about her, the good and the bad, as she needed to know about him.

One of her lists was headed *If Marriage Not Possible*, and contained several ideas for explaining a baby to the neighbours. The top one being that she was already

89

pregnant when Robert died. Lower down the list was the story that it was her sisters or cousins orphaned child.

From the remoteness of the telephone Philip said, 'I'm sorry about lunchtime Jean. I should have been more understanding. I'll come on Friday. I'll leave the car a couple of streets away and walk. I'll say it's an insurance job with the people only available in the evenings.'

Jean sighed deeply when she replaced the receiver. For a while this afternoon she had thought that Philip had no intention of marrying her. She saw enough of it in her work - the other woman who existed on promises, and she vowed never to be in that position. Of course if she wasn't in such a state about her condition she would not have doubted him at all. She realised this and included it in her reasonings. Friday was two days away, but so sure was she now about the pregnancy that it never crossed her mind that maybe she wouldn't have such dire news to impart by then.

She prepared a meal for two when she arrived home from work on that Friday. She was nervous, but composed. Nervous because she knew how he liked his life planned, even as she did, and she had already decided that however difficult this was going to be, nothing should deny this new life that was forming inside her. Composed because she had set the scene in her mind and knew where she was going.

She told him matter of factly, almost as though she was discussing a business deal. 'Philip, the night we spent near Windsor - quite unexpectedly really?'

'Yes.' His smile gave his features a softer charm.

'I'm pretty sure I'm pregnant. I've not seen a doctor yet, wanted to tell you first, but I'll make an appointment for next week.'

He looked shattered. The one thing she had not allowed for in her calculations was that she had had time to become used to the idea and he had not.

'Oh Jean, I hope not.' In the circumstances it wasn't the best remark to make.

'*You* hope not. What do you think I do? I'm the one who's going to carry the can, I'm the one whose work will go, whose reputation will go, whose whole life will be turned upside down. *And you hope not.*'

He was very contrite. 'Darling, don't worry, between us we'll think of something.'

'I've already thought. I shall have the baby, I couldn't do otherwise Philip. And I've made a list of possible actions...' she handed him three pieces of cardboard used in stocking and tight packets. 'Here, these are the alternatives.'

He read them solemnly, and equally solemnly tore them up.

'What do you think you're doing?'

'There are no alternatives Jean. It's a shock I admit - but what's done is done. We'll simply marry sooner than we would have.'

'How can we?' Her voice was sharp with anxiety and fear.

'I'll tell Sonia about the baby. I know her well enough to know she won't hold out against that. She'll want the child to come into the world having two parents who are married. She is very moral,' he added as she looked disbelievingly at him.

'I'd better - check with the doctor. Oh I know it's true, but before you do anything I'll get official confirmation.'

Suddenly life went at a terrific pace. Always in the past Jean had been organised for almost every possibility; now she never knew what to expect next. The doctor told her the baby was due in February - if Philip wasn't free long before then she would start to show.

'Philip, I think I'm very moral too,' she said one day. 'I want to let people think this is my husband's baby.'

'That's not being moral, it's being snobbish and narrow.'

'But...'

'Of course it is. It's *my* baby and we shall be married as soon as we can. If you can't face the neighbours you'll have to move. That might be a good idea anyway, because Sonia will keep our house. It's still on a mortgage of course, but she'll be able to manage because she's working too. She may even sell up and find something smaller, although that's not easy is it?'

'You mean we find somewhere for us and I live in it until you're free to come?'

'That's about it.'

'Yes, I think I will. Maybe I'm a coward Philip. It's me I'm thinking about as much as the child you know.'

Life became very busy. She and Robert had been renting the house, and she thought if they could begin by renting again it would be better. Philip however wanted to buy. 'I've insurances to take care of the deposit,' he said, 'and in any case working for the bank gives me many advantages. The house must be near enough to my job, although it doesn't have to be central. I don't mind half an hours' drive - how about you, any preferences?'

'I don't think we'll have a lot of choice, Philip.'

'Once we're married and settled I'll try for promotion. Out of London. Do you fancy a small country town?'

'Sounds fine to me, darling, especially now we're starting a family.'

'Yes. Put all this behind us. Oh Jean, if *only* I'd met you first.'

She poured over estate agents leaflets, spent Saturdays dashing around to look at properties, and began to blossom to such an extent that the talk in the office was that she had met someone else and was in love.

Philip's wife ran true to the form Philip had said she would and not only didn't contest the divorce, but made everything as easy as she could for them, and Jean moved from her house at the beginning of September. She had told no-one of her condition, and if her friends and neighbours thought she had put on a little weight they kept those thoughts to themselves. Her local friends had in any case been hers and not joint ones with Robert for many years, and the older ones whom they had known together she wrote to give her new address.

Philip bought the house in his name, although she insisted on paying her share of the deposit too. 'I have enough money, and later, when we're married we can have it transferred to a joint contract or whatever.'

The move went well. Philip was leaving all but his own special books and bringing nothing in the way of furniture, so she simply took all of hers. He appeared at eight o clock in the evening on the day of the move.

'How did it go darling? I'm just sorry I couldn't be here to help you, but leave the unpacking of everything except essentials until I can be. You mustn't overdo things.'

'It wasn't too bad really, and already the lady next door has introduced herself. She seems a good sort. Said she simply wanted me to know she was there should I need anything, which was rather nice. I think we'll be OK here darling.'

Within two months Philip had joined her. She had subtly let it be known that her 'husband' was working away and could only get home occasionally, which accounted for the times his car was in the drive. The divorce went through and a week later Jean and Philip were married and beginning to look forward again.

From never imagining herself a mother, even when she was expecting the first time, - 'I don't know why,' she said to Philip, 'but I really never thought I should be, nor to be honest have I ever hankered after maternity,' - she found herself revelling in her forthcoming role, and taking part with enthusiasm in the choosing of colours not only for the rest of the house, but particularly for the nursery.

Chapter 8

'Mmm, that was good.' Julien smacked his lips in appreciation of the meal he had just eaten. 'Now you sit and relax and I'll make a drink. Tea or coffee?'

She smiled across to him, 'Coffee for me please, then I'll tell you about my day. Can face it more with that lct inside me.'

He kissed her tenderly, then, clearing the plates from the table went off to the kitchen area and Daisy sank into the only armchair in the room and closed her eyes. It was comforting to hear the sound of cups being placed onto saucers, the chink of metal spoon against china, and the faint buzz as Julien poured the water. As he walked towards her, the whiff of coffee made her open her eyes.

'Only instant tonight, but in cups not mugs. We'll get our culinary arrangements sorted out as soon as we can.' he said, drawing one of the dining chairs next to her, 'you fire away whenever you're ready.'

'It was very disappointing.' she said. 'Perhaps I expected too much, but no-one recognised me. Not a soul.'

'What did you tell them?'

'That I was looking for a job. I said, in each case, that I had been living in the country and teaching ballet. It was awkward when they asked for qualifications, and I felt terrible lying to them, but I did as we planned and told them our house had been burgled and my certificates stolen. Then I mentioned, I hope vaguely, the main ones we looked up the other day. The ones they would expect

95

me to have. They didn't question them. I suppose it isn't the sort of thing people usually lie about.'

'In any case, with or without certificates, they would want to see you dance I imagine.' Julien laid his arm across her shoulders. 'Go on.'

'One of them asked me to audition there and then. I did and they said they would let me know when they had a vacancy. And I've an audition with another next week, but again they aren't looking for anyone at the moment, it's just for future possibilities.' She sipped her coffee. 'Maybe I wasn't a ballet dancer, Julien, in spite of our surmises.'

'You must have had something to do with that world my love, you wouldn't be as good as you are at it if not. Perhaps you taught and aren't so far from the truth after all. You may not have been a performer.'

'Yet I also know complete ballets so well.'

'That follows because you went to see them anyway.'

She sighed deeply, 'I suppose I was hoping to be able to say to you tonight that someone had recognised me, called me by my name. In my happiest dream I would have told you that when she did I recalled everything, and in a slightly lesser dream, that even if I didn't remember, someone out there in the world knew who I was and all about me.'

Julien left for work soon after eight each morning, and although she met him for lunch a couple of times during those first weeks in London, it was too rushed an affair to be pleasant, and in the crowded cafes and sandwich bars there was no chance for private conversation, indeed for any conversation at all, and they stopped doing so. It made a long day. When she had exhausted the ballet and theatre companies she wondered where to look next.

Maybe I had better find a job and forget about trying to discover my past,' she said one evening. In any case I shall need to earn some money. I can't go on the dole, not without a proper identity.'

They looked at each other for what was only seconds yet seemed to her like many minutes. Then she turned away. She knew what he wanted to say. She read it in his eyes, the plea for her to publicise her loss of memory and encourage knowledge from outside, and she tried not to cringe at the thought but it was no use. Somehow she couldn't bring herself to do this and it puzzled her. After all, she argued with herself, if I have such a retiring nature how is it that I enjoyed teaching the children. Standing out front demonstrating the steps I wasn't self-conscious. I wasn't worried, embarrassed, afraid. Is it fear now that prevents me from agreeing to what I know he thinks is an obvious answer? A shiver rippled through her body and Julien held his hands out to her.

'You know I only want what's best for you, darling. If you can do that, work and leave the memory thing to sort itself out or not, without fretting.'

'That's the trouble really, isn't it Julien? I do fret and worry over who I am, what I was doing on that train, but most of all that there is no clue anywhere. It's almost as if I didn't exist before.'

'I believe you're trying too hard Daisy. I know you do put it out of your mind, but you do this consciously, not naturally. Easy for me to say a thing like that I suppose, but if you really could forget and push it right to the back of your mind, you might – what is it? What did I say? He looked at her in amazement, for she was rocking back and forth with laughter, a frenzied kind of sound that shook her whole body.

'Forget, forget – that is the problem, isn't it? I can forget easily enough, it's remembering I'm having trouble with. Oh…' and as Julien rushed over and took her in his arms, her strange laughter turned to tears and sobs that racked her whole frame.

'Darling, darling, don't upset yourself so. Please. I didn't mean it, you must know I wouldn't deliberately do or say anything to hurt you. Daisy, please, please try to stop.' But she couldn't. It seemed that once started, as that other time when Sarah's taunts had produced a similar outburst, she was powerless to halt the cascade of tears that poured from her eyes, and the brittle, breathless sobs that escaped through her lips.

Julien cuddled her, he stroked and kissed her, trying to comfort her as one might a child, yet still it went on. 'Hush darling,' he whispered, 'or we'll disturb Mrs Jones or one of the others. They'll wonder what I'm doing to you.'

Eventually, through sheer exhaustion her crying eased. She looked spent and Julien picked her up bodily and carried her through to the bedroom. He helped her undress, slipped her nightgown over her head, then said softly, 'I'll pop upstairs for some things, then I'll be back. I won't leave you tonight. Don't worry sweetheart, nothing will happen, not this time. I shall simply be here with you.'

She slept fitfully. Each time she woke Julien stirred. He had brought a sleeping bag down with him and he spread it on the floor next to the bed.

'Julien there's no need for that, you know,' she said.

'There's not room for two of us in that little bed.' He grinned, then said seriously, 'if you get frightened again just yell out.'

She looked fragile in the morning, but there had been no more tears or strange laughter. Over breakfast she apologised for being a burden.

'None of that sort of talk, we love each other. He almost said remember, and stopped just in time. 'Maybe it's a good thing it happened. Get some of the frustration out of your system. I have tried to imagine how it would be Daisy. It isn't easy when you haven't experienced it. Easier perhaps to visualise what it would be like to be blind or deaf, but together we'll beat it my love, I know we will, and we'll build new memories, our memories.'

Her face seemed to tremble a little as she smiled at him and reached out her hand. 'Dear Julien,' she said, 'dear, dear Julien.'

When he had left for work Daisy washed and tidied the flat, then she sat at the table with two sheets of writing paper before her. On one she wrote across the top in large printed letters THINGS I KNOW. On the other a question mark. The list for the positive side, the things I know column, grew encouragingly. Dancing, music

99

(especially with a beat) coffee, plain chocolate, savoury biscuits, the colour green... she rapidly covered the sheet of paper and turned it over. Then she stopped and reread the list. It's all *things*, she thought Things I like or know I like. There is nothing there that I know about my life. Nothing like my fears, my religion, my hates and loves. Well, what do you fear, she asked herself. Stop right now and think about it.

Mice, spiders, snakes, there had been something in the paper only the other day about somebody who had a phobia about them. None of them made her shudder. True she was only looking at the words and thinking about them, not seeing or having to handle one, yet, although she didn't want to touch any of them, they didn't repulse her, and they certainly didn't frighten her. There she was again, going for things, the definite article. What about abstract fears?

Her head was aching now and leaving the papers on the table she rose and went to make herself some coffee. While she was boiling the kettle and spooning the powder into the cup the answer came to her. She was afraid of herself, afraid in case her past had not been lily white. Afraid to discover why she was on that train without a single identifying item on her. And all the time she stayed afraid she would not remember.

Perhaps that too is the reason I won't tell anyone I'm suffering from amnesia she thought. Is it really guilt at losing my memory because I think it is my own fault. Is that why I refuse to advertise my loss and allow people to help me? The first glimmer of excitement, and yes, maybe it was hope too, tingled through her veins.

'That's what I have to do,' she said aloud, 'find out about me. Not the material things I like or dislike, but the real things. The me that I was and probably still am – the inside me. Then I'll probably remember all the rest. Who I was married to, why nobody has taken the trouble to find out if I'm dead or alive...'

Julien found her calm and pale when he returned from work. 'Did you take it easy today?' he asked, gazing at her anxiously.

'Yes. Did quite a lot of thinking too. I know now what I shall do next, Julien.'

His arm came round her. 'Yes?'

'I'm going to start my own dancing school. That is if I can find a hall somewhere.'

The idea was good, she thought, several days later, but the practicality of it probably wasn't. For a start she had to find a suitable hall - not an easy task. The few that were available it seemed, were so pricy she didn't even consider them. And of course she had to pay, in advance, before she knew if she had anyone to teach.

'Find your pupils first,' Julien advised, 'and give them a starting date, say a month hence.'

'I don't know about that; if a little girl wants to learn to dance she wants to be able to come immediately I think. It's too risky. I mean, suppose I gather six or seven and then can't book a room?'

101

'The decision has to be yours of course my darling, but wouldn't it be easier to get a job as a dancing teacher in an existing school? Why the urge to have your own one so quickly?'

She turned her gaze away from his eyes. 'I think it's because I can't face the hassle of principals wanting to see certificates. Of them needing to know where I last worked, why I left, where I was living, all the bits and pieces which would normally be taken for granted. If I'm the governor then I'm not answerable to anyone except myself.'

'And the taxman, if you do as well as I'm sure you will,' he said with a wicked grin.

She pulled a face at him. 'Ah well, I'll tackle that one when it arises.'

A religion still bothered her. Ever since she had thought deeply about the subject she felt she should know, and to this end she began visiting churches of different denominations around London. When the search for a hall reached a point when she didn't know where to look next, she turned her attention to the churches.

She began by wandering in and looking round. If there was a priest there she often talked to him. It was strange, this ease with which she spoke to the clergy. Maybe it's their anonymity, she thought, behind the robe or dog collar was also an unknown quantity, as indeed she was. But the part of them that showed their calling was there to help. She never asked for help of course - never even told them what was troubling her, but she looked around their churches and asked intelligent questions about them. Yet she could not bring herself to talk to them about their beliefs. She felt as at home in Westminster Abbey and St. Paul's Cathedral as she did in the smaller churches of the capital; perhaps it had more to do with the holy atmosphere than with her personal religion, she thought.

She began going to the services with Julien. He wasn't keen at first, but he agreed to accompany her, and so, several evenings a week they would smarten up and attend evensong at a different rendezvous. Daisy found comfort in them all. 'I don't know if it's the words, the atmosphere, the buildings, I simply don't know,' she said, 'but it helps me. I know afterwards that I have to keep on searching for myself, and I know that I shall succeed. It gives me a kind of peace too, a continuity Julien, to realise that for thousands of years others have sat and knelt here.'

'Well you've tried almost everything now dear,' he said one Sunday as they walked home from another service, 'It only leaves the synagogue and Mormon Temple.'

'The synagogue...'

'No'. Julien was unexpectedly firm. 'I will come with you to a service once, twice a week, but that's all. You're using it as a prop Daisy, you must see that. If you really believe then a prayer said by the side of your bed at night would give you the same relief.'

Hurt by his words she struck back. 'It doesn't. I've tried. But in the church there's the music, in some there's

103

candles, there's the words, the prayers, and there's someone leading them, showing you which way to go. On my own I'm stumbling, trying to find an answer.'

'Very well. But not every night my love. It's becoming an obsession.'

Yet it was through her interest in churches that she found the hall for her dancing school. Despondent after chasing three that particular day, none of which were suitable - one being a dark basement, smaller than advertised, with poor lighting and no facilities at all, she turned into St. Stephens Church. The door was locked, and, her disappointment acute she walked down a different path going in the opposite direction without realising it, and found herself among the old gravestones. She could see a smaller gate leading into another street and when she emerged, there abutting the back of the church was the hall. The door was partly open, so gently she pushed it a little more and went inside.

'Good afternoon. Can I help you?' The voice was pleasing, a slight accent gave it interest, although she couldn't immediately pinpoint the area.

It wasn't very light in there, and she looked round as a tall, athletic looking man came towards her.

'Hullo. I'm Jim. And you are?'

'Daisy. Daisy Shore.'

'Welcome Daisy. Can I assist you in any way. I'm sort of connected with the church and the hall. The vicar's an old school chum of mine, and I run the youth club here.'

'W-ell...' Her mind worked rapidly. 'What I'm really looking for is a hall to use as a dance centre for young people. Really young people I mean. I want to run a ballet class you see, but everywhere suitable is either booked up for years to come, or much too expensive for me to hire.' She was gazing round as she spoke, assessing the possibilities.

'You had better have a word with David. He's the vicar. He'll do his best to help I can assure you. And he won't overcharge. If you can agree on a suitable night, or afternoon I suppose you'll need if its young children you're teaching...'

She nodded eagerly. 'Where can I find David - the vicar, I mean?'

Jim glanced at his watch. 'Probably at home right now, having a bite to eat before coming round to us this evening. He usually looks in and spends an hour with the boys on youth club nights. If you can hang on for a few minutes while I finish the preparations in here, I'll show you where he lives. It's not far,' he added.

The vicarage was less than five minutes away, and David, the vicar of St. Stephens seemed as nice and uncomplicated as his friend Jim.

'One afternoon a week. I should think we could manage that,' he said, smiling at her. 'How much could you pay?'

Incredibly, after weeks and weeks of frustration, it all seemed to be coming together. She had a hall, at a reasonable rent, not too far away; now she had to find some pupils.

She began the search by advertising on the local newsagent's board of cards in the window. Then, a little further afield, she did the same thing in another newsagent. She also went to the library and asked them if they would display a card on their counter. 'Nothing big and cumbersome,' she said, 'just a simple notice about the new dancing school.'

And the applications rolled in. All the little girls of the area, it seemed, were waiting for just such an opportunity to learn to dance.

Within three weeks of finding the hall she had a class of eleven children. True the girls outnumbered the boys - nine to two, but she was in business. As they were all between five and eight years of age, she was able to make it one class. Later, she thought, if the school grows I will have a babies class and an older one. Or a beginners and an advanced. But all that was in the future; a future that looked better now each day.

She held her dancing lessons between four and five o clock. That gave mums time to collect the children from school and bring them to St. Stephen's Hall. Most of the mums waited, sitting on small wooden chairs lining the sides of the hall, and intermittently smiling at their offspring as they wobbled unsteadily into the various positions Daisy outlined. But some of the parents left the children and returned an hour later to collect them.

A few of the children might make dancers if they kept it up, but for the majority it would be a fun thing, and, as she said to Julien, marvellous for future deportment.

It was satisfying working out the programme, and organising her affairs. Sometimes she thought it gave her a pleasure out of all proportion to what was involved, and realised it was because this was something she knew about right from the beginning; something *she* had begun. There was no guesswork here, and she admitted to herself the wonder of the freedom she felt because of it.

The school progressed and in December she decided to organise a Christmas concert for the parents and other relatives and friends they cared to bring. Basing her ballet on the nativity, she soon injected her enthusiasm into the little ones, who practised harder than ever to be good 'on the night'. A slight problem arose when it came to choosing the three kings. With only two boys in the class, one of them was Joseph and the other the Innkeeper. Laughingly she told Julien about it, 'Three of the tallest girls are to be the kings, but they would all much rather be angels, because as Christine said, 'Kings are boys and angels are girls.'

'I told her they may not be - why not a boy angel, but she shook her head and said sadly, "Angels wear dresses Miss." '

The obvious choice to play Mary was the least talented dancer, for Mary would be sitting by her Baby and rocking the cradle most of the time. The child who qualified for that title was blue-eyed, fair haired, a real little model girl. Daisy knew that another child, seven year old Debra who was completely opposite to her in looks and demeanour was *aching* to be Mary. Debra had straight brown shoulder length hair, a bit ragged at the ends, and sometimes Daisy itched to give it a proper cut. She wore round flesh coloured national health glasses, and although she was improving in her movements, her hands and arms often didn't look as though they belonged to the rest of her.

'Point your arm towards *that* corner, Debra,' Daisy would say, in an effort to get them all going in the same direction. 'That's better, uncurl your hand and point that too dear...' usually by then Debra had lost her balance, so they started over again. Yet once she had mastered the movement, Debra was brilliant, doing it over and over until she had it perfectly. They had all done the angels dance which Daisy composed - simple but effective, or it would be when they had their proper costumes with shimmering wings, and Debra, by sheer hard practice was now by far the best in the class at it. However - she knew that she would cast Debra as Mary, because the child may never have another chance.

Her reward was the love which shone from Debra's eyes and face when she looked at her.

Julien promised to come to the performance - one only, three nights before Christmas; meanwhile Daisy stitched and glued, and found a degree of satisfaction in working with her hands. 'Something else I didn't know I enjoyed,' she said to Julien as she laid the final crown beside the others on the table.

He picked it up carefully and examined it. 'Mmm, not at all bad', he said, grinning at her. 'Perhaps you were a playschool teacher, or even a presenter on *Blue Peter*...' he ducked as she threw a cushion at his head.

Yet she felt good that they could joke about her lack of memory so easily now. It was almost a part of their conversation, and it took some of the tenseness from her. She was still tremendously uptight when others were present, and sometimes this too bothered her. After all, she told herself in the privacy of her bed, if I never recover those lost years I don't want to go through the rest of my life with a huge chip on my shoulder, and I know, without the reminders Julien sometimes lets out, that I am ultra-sensitive over it...

They were to spend Christmas back in Torquay, dividing their time between his family and Jill and Ian. Strangely she was looking forward to it with some misgivings. Maybe because she had been thrown onto her own resources for the last three months. Yet it would be good to see them again, for since her departure in October none of them had managed to get to town, nor she to Torquay. Sarah had planned a weekend, and there were excited telephone calls about it, but eventually that hadn't materialised because she caught flu, and all her other weekends seemed to be booked.

Once a week Daisy telephoned them from the payphone in the hall, and although she always chose a time when it seemed everyone in the flats was out, she knew she must sound reticent over the telephone, for she was ever conscious that it was very far from private.

The letters were a wonderful lifeline - a link with the only past she remembered, and Daisy read and reread every one, and then kept them in a shoebox. Jill's were usually several pages long, written in a flowing, sloping manner, and full of chat about the family, the house, and

109

the town; what she was currently making for Christmas decoration, and the soft toy class she had joined.

Sarah had written several letters in a round, clear, almost childish hand, seven and eight pages long, detailing her latest love - "what I ever saw in that other lout I'll never know!" And she had answered them in equal length and depth of feeling, glad that for Sarah she hadn't been a passing whim, a novelty. And with a tiny glow somewhere inside her that she had been able to help Sarah through a difficult phase in her growing up.

Chapter 9

They travelled to Torquay the day before Christmas Eve, after Julian finished work. She insisted on going with him to the ticket office in case anything should ring a bell in her mind about that fateful journey in the spring. Nothing did. It was raining, the station was packed, and as she followed Julien through the barrier and onto their train, tears pricked her eyes.

They managed to find seats together and Julien lifted their luggage to the rack, then sank down beside her. 'Well we made it sweetheart. Didn't fancy standing all that way. Daisy, what is it my love? He took hold of her hand and squeezed it gently and lovingly.

'Nothing really. That's the trouble, absolutely nothing. I hoped that somehow, somewhere along this route to the station, the ticket office, boarding the train, a train from London to Torquay, something might have sparked a memory, but it hasn't. I may have been here dozens of times before, but I still can't recall that last time.'

'Daisy, what can I say? I want you to remember every bit as much as you want to, believe me darling I do. But equally it doesn't matter. We can build our life, our memories, together. We've already started and it can only get better. But I do understand how much you want to *know*, and if there was a way, if it was humanly possible for me to help you regain the past, you know I would. Darling, let's look forward as much as we can. Soon it will be a new year, a new beginning.'

She swallowed several times to rid herself of the lump that kept rising in her throat. 'I know dear, and I didn't mean to harp on it. Somehow it just caught up with me, but from this moment on it's only the future that counts.'

'That's my girl.'

It was truly lovely to be back. After the initial hugging Jill held her at arms' length and eyed her critically. 'You're thinner. Are you eating properly Daisy?'

'Yes of course I am, but I do a workout every day now in the dancing school, that's probably why. We eat rather well, usually one night in Julien's place and one night in mine.'

'Sarah will be in soon, she's out doing some last minute shopping. Oh and Pam from the dancing school phoned a couple of days ago to know when you were to be here. Said she hopes you'll have time to go round for a Christmas drink, both of you of course'

Daisy sighed deeply with contentment. She had made friends with Janice, the young woman from one of the flats in the neighbouring house in London, and she knew casually the parents of her dancing children, but these friends from the summer were very special to her. They had not forgotten. Both Pam and Maudie kept in touch by letter, and knew she was coming down for Christmas.

'It's like coming home,' she said, forcing back the emotion that threatened to engulf her again. Sarah made no secret of her delight in having Daisy there, and it did her heart good to be so wanted

'I'll bring Darren in to meet you,' she said, 'we've been together almost three months now. That's something of a record for me, and I'm actually still in love with him.'

On the morning of Christmas Eve Julian went to see his parents and Daisy visited Pam, before joining him there for lunch. She was overwhelmed by the naturalness of it all. Alison threw her arms around her and pleaded to be allowed to sit next to her at table.

'She was afraid you weren't coming after all when Julian arrived this morning without you,' Anne whispered in an aside, 'and that would have quite spoilt her Christmas I know.'

'Tell us about your dancing school. Are there any girls called Alison there? Do they dance better than me?'

'Hush Alison, and stop firing questions at Daisy. Let her get her breath, then she'll tell us all her exciting news.' Daisy laughed, then launched into the story of how she found the hall and began the Daisy Shore Dancing Academy.

'The Christmas Concert was fun and went off quite well. The mums and dads brought neighbours and aunts and uncles, the vicar and the youth club leader who was instrumental in finding the hall for me really, came, so the children had a reasonable size audience. They lapped it up, all behaved like veterans of the theatre, and not one of them over eight years old.'

It was a happy few hours, and Alison clung to Daisy's hand when they were leaving. Julian separated them and swung his niece high in the air, 'She'll be back the day after tomorrow. Now you be good and go to bed early tonight, because you know who's coming, don't you?' He lowered her to the ground, and taking Daisy's hand in his, hurried down the path with her.

The plan was to spend Christmas Day with Jill and Ian and Boxing Day with Julian's parents, so they visited Maude that evening. She hadn't been well for several weeks.

'Nothing particular,' she told them, 'me rheumatics been playing up a bit, and all this rain we've had hasn't helped. If I won the pools I'd probably go abroad to an island in the sun for the winter, then I'd live to be a hundred.' She laughed, 'There now, you don't want to hear about my aches and pains, tell me all your news instead.'

Walking home along the seafront later that night, with Julian's arm comfortingly around her shoulders Daisy said, 'She's nice, isn't she? Yet when I first met her I thought she was a nosy old woman. I know I said I wouldn't, but I can't help thinking what she said about memories. I'm glad she can look back to her happy times without resentment that they are no longer there. Listening to her you know makes me feel ashamed that I grumble. She's had a rough passage in life and as she said this time of year everything seems enhanced, the good and the bad.'

Later, in bed in her old room at the Humphreys, she felt too wide awake to sleep, and her mind returned as it always did when she was alone, to that past that eluded her. Memory plays such a role in all our lives, she thought. Happy memories and sad memories, grey and blue memories, and there is such an awful gap when there are *no* memories.

Turning over in bed she resolutely closed her eyes and visualised her class of children doing their exercises – one, two, three, one, two, three, to the right, down, to the left, up, one, two, three, one, two... her muscles relaxed and she slept.

When Jill and Ian realised Maude Church would be alone for Christmas they immediately invited her over for the day, and so at nine o clock on Christmas morning Ian and Daisy drove to fetch her. It was a happy holiday, they all went to the morning service at the church round the corner, and once again Daisy felt the companionship of being in the hallowed building. She hugged the warm affability to herself and said nothing of her pleasure to the others for fear of – of what? Ridicule? No, not that, but perhaps a gentle teasing that her imagination was working overtime. Maybe it was at that, but increasingly her need was answered by those moments in a church.

It was a happy dinner party, a relaxed afternoon, and, because the rain had stopped, a short walk along the front before tea. In the evening they played games, and Maudie laughed until tears ran down her cheeks at Daisy's attempts at portraying Andy Capp, in one of the charades they did. It was much later when Daisy wondered how she knew what Andy Capp looked like, and briefly thought that it proved her memory *was* there, behind the cloud that descended with the train crash.

Julien returned to London after Christmas, but Daisy stayed on in Torquay. She wasn't certain how long for, her room in town was paid until the end of January, and she felt more ready now to tackle the problem of the other unidentified people from the crash. She realised that had the police known she was suffering from amnesia they would have questioned her further at the time and after. She said a silent prayer for Doctor Plymouth and Ian and Jill's protection over that,

Julien was due back at work for two days, then off again for the New Year, and she spent the time without him with Maude, Pam and of course Jill, Ian and Sarah. She met Sarah's new boyfriend, Darren, who seemed a pleasant enough lad, and who certainly treated Sarah with more courtesy than her last love had.

She and Julien, Jill and Ian, and Ethel and Arthur, Julien's parents, went together for a meal on New Year's Eve. They went to one of the hotels where they were also able to enjoy a cabaret and a brief spell of dancing to the resident band. All too soon it seemed, the festivities were over and she was seeing Julien off on the train back to town, and returning to Murray House with the sobering thought that tomorrow she must start investigations into the unidentified victims of last spring's train crash. If, by now, the police had found out who they were, maybe she could begin her own enquiries with their families to see if she belonged to any of them. She knew she would not marry Julien until her identity was solved, even if she never recalled it herself, and it worried her beyond Julien's comprehension that she was carrying on a life and taking on other commitments before she knew what she already had.

116

She felt nervous when she went into the police station on that bleak January morning. When she had explained her mission to the sergeant at the desk he asked her to wait while he contacted someone else. Sitting on a chair she gazed around at the other two people already there – a young man about seventeen or eighteen, with long untidy hair and an unshaven face, and a ginger haired girl about the same age and very obviously pregnant. They seemed to be together, and she realised with a pang how much she wanted to be with Julien again. She missed him more than she realised she would. Was it because he made her feel secure? With him she was part of a twosome, never completely alone even in her thoughts, because he was now so involved in her life. I do love him, she thought. I would never contemplate being here now if I didn't, but I mustn't blind myself to the fact that I hate having no-one of my own. Did I always feel like this I wonder, or is it a side effect of the amnesia? Have I ever loved anyone else? She twisted the bright gold band which she still wore on the third finger of her left hand. Someone, sometime, had placed it there, and until she knew who, and what had happened to him, she could not marry Julien, no matter how much in love they were.

'Would you come this way please?' The sergeant smiled across to her, and she jumped up and followed him into an interview room. 'Sergeant Jameson will be with you in a moment,' he said as he went out and closed the door.

'And everyone was accounted for Daisy?' Sarah gazed across the dinner table at her.

'Yes. They grumbled at me for not telling them before about not remembering who I was, but they were all very understanding at the police station. Especially when I said I had expected my memory to return, that I thought it was simply shock. I never mentioned the hospital or anything of course.'

'So where do you go from here?' Ian poured more wine into her glass, and she lifted her eyebrows at him.

'I really don't know, Ian. Maybe I should contact these people who lost someone in the crash, but you know I don't think I can. I mean, I obviously don't belong to any of them or they would have tried to find me. It's an absolute mystery. I must have been up to no good, or I would have had some form of identification on me surely.'

'That does seem odd I agree, but doubtless there was a reason, which, when we know who you are, will probably come to light.'

'Maybe you don't *want* to remember. I mean there's all sorts of reasons I can think of as to why you may, subconsciously deny its return,' Sarah joined in.

'I know, and it's very frightening. What is the longest anyone has gone in this state, Ian?' she asked suddenly.

'I don't really know my dear. And that isn't a fobbing off, I haven't dealt with many cases of amnesia before. Never anything like yours.'

'You must have thought about it. Formed your own ideas about it. I mean I am perfectly fit now, completely

118

over any shock from the crash itself. Tell me a bit about the condition Ian. I don't know, but it might help.'

'Yes, I've thought about it, and looked it up since of course, but I can't produce a cure. You have a *severe* pre-traumatic amnesia, which simply means loss of memory of things before the accident. In view of the lack of serious injury to yourself I would say it is a sort of hysterical type of memory loss. Now that doesn't mean you are a hysterical person you understand...'

'The puzzling thing is why there were no documents. Most people have something, either in their bag or on their person, to identify them,' Jill said, 'but now you are actively delving, something may turn up Daisy dear.'

'I hope so,' she said fervently. 'I ought to have followed it up a lot sooner than this I know, but I couldn't bring myself to, and now, when I need to know for legal purposes maybe too long has elapsed.'

She paid one more visit to the police station before returning to London. It was a strange situation, for here she was, to all intents a healthy person, yet with something missing that most people took for granted. At least now I am beginning to look at it more dispassionately, she thought, and that can only be a help.

She was asked to leave her name and present address in case there were any enquiries, or any evidence about her turned up, as the sergeant rather cryptically put it. It seemed doubtful to her that anyone would try to find her now, seven months afterwards. No, if they were interested in her welfare, any family or friends she might have had would have been in touch long ago.

119

'Depends,' the sergeant said, sucking his lower lip, something she noticed he did quite often.

'On what, Sergeant Jameson?'

'Your family may be abroad. You may not have been a frequent letter writer, oh, there's all sorts of possibilities, and as Christmas is just behind us, if they haven't heard from you they may try to get in touch. When they find you have disappeared they may contact us, or our equivalent wherever you lived before, and that way we shall be able to reunite you all.'

'You make it sound so easy,' she said, 'you even make it seem possible.'

'It is, Mrs Shore, it is.' He rose and opened the door for her.

Chapter 10

Back in London January seemed bleak. Coming from the warmth of her welcome in Torquay she felt bereft after Julien had left for work in the mornings. The dancing school was not due to begin again for another week, and it was too cold to wander for long in the parks and squares that were one of her greatest delights. She felt safe with the houses all around her, and had even begun to write a ballet where the dancers, representing Londoners through the ages, sped or sauntered among the trees and gracious houses in various London Squares. In her imagination she saw them on stage, in the dress of the period they were portraying, a different scene for each era, right up to the present day, when the fine houses, the ladies and gentlemen, maids, butlers and cooks, had given way to flats and flatlets, and the modern folk who lived in them. But although she would have liked to put on her own production, it was far from being the main dream...

The night before the academy opened again Julien said, 'Let's go out and see a show Daisy. I've got tickets for *Fun and Games Not Allowed*. It's supposed to be very funny, and I reckon a bit of light heartedness would do us both good, don't you?'

She didn't really feel like turning out for the theatre, but as Julien had the tickets, and so obviously wanted to take her out of herself she agreed.

They ate before the show in a little Italian restaurant, and were settled in their seats at the theatre when Julien

121

suddenly said, 'A drink in the interval, shall I go and order one darling, it will save the crush, and the wait, later?'

When he had gone Daisy gazed around her and watched the people filing in and finding their seats. She found herself gazing into faces, wondering what their lives were like. If they were happy with their lot or wanted to change it. For surely she must have been unhappy and wanting change to have been on a train without any identification at all. It was the only logical thing *she could* think, because nowadays she never went anywhere without her diary with her name, albeit a fictional one, and address in it. It seemed that you could make intelligent guesses as far as that, but then... nothing. You needed to know something about yourself to know what you were running from.

'Gosh there's a crowd in that bar now. All drinking as if there's no tomorrow,' Julien said, as he sat beside her a few moments later. 'Here, I bought a programme.'

It *was* a funny play and Daisy really did forget her worries for an hour as she became immersed in the antics of the actors and actresses on the stage. When the curtain came down for the interval they made their way to the bar and their reserved drinks. It was noisy and they stood just outside in the passage, quietly smiling at each other.

'Enjoying it darling?'

She nodded. 'Very much. You were right, a light hearted play was just the tonic I needed. I'm becoming much too introspective since Christmas and the police station visit.'

122

They both liked the theatre, but in spite of her words Daisy couldn't help wondering, as she revelled in the colour and gaiety of the audience as they went in and out of the bar, whether she had been a regular theatregoer before, or if she had spent all her time the other side of the footlights.

The second half was as hilarious as the first and they were both still laughing as they made their way down the stairs and into the foyer. Someone bumped her gently.

'Sorry.' The woman smiled, 'Hullo Clare.' She was gone even as Daisy turned to look.

She tried to follow, dragging Julien with her, but it was no use. People were spilling out of all doors and into the foyer. Rushing in the direction the woman had taken simply led to another exit and the pavement. Desperately she searched for that face again. All she could recall was a cloud of dark hair.

'Julien, quickly, we've got to find her - that woman, *she knew me*.' She pulled him back inside, getting tangled with the people streaming out, and began darting about, peering at every woman she could.

'Daisy, come along dear.'

'But she knew me Julien. I've got to find her again. Help me, for God's sake help me.'

'Sshh, keep your voice down.'

'Clare, she called me Clare. Clare.' She said the word again and again. 'Oh where did she go? You should have stopped her, grabbed her and hung on until I could ask her, and now she could be anywhere. In a taxi, speeding away somewhere out of my reach, and she's the *only* one

123

who's ever shown any recognition...' she was crying now, and Julien took hold of her arm quite roughly and edged her outside.

'No, Julien, no.'

'Be quiet, you're making an exhibition of yourself. She's gone, and it's too late for that particular clue. It's a shame Daisy, but it's not the end of the world. Now pull yourself together for goodness sake and let's go home.'

She alternately sobbed and raged at Julien when they finally reached their flats. He made some coffee, and tried to convince her that if one person recognised her there would be others, and they must therefore go to the theatre oftener - 'not the ballet, but other kinds of theatre.'

'And I suppose you think I'll have the luck for someone else to bump into me and then recognise me,' she cried scathingly.

Julien sighed. 'No of course not, but if we mingle there's always a chance and so far we've been more to the ballet or the serious plays.'

'Go away, go away, you don't understand, you don't even try to understand any more...'

He left when he had drunk his coffee. Standing by the door he said 'I'm trying to help. What happened tonight was one of those chance things that could happen again. And at least you know one positive thing now - that your name is Clare. Although if this is how you behave as Clare I'd rather have Daisy.' The door clicked quietly and she was alone.

She didn't see him the following morning. Usually he looked in on his way to work. I suppose I did make a bit of a spectacle of myself, she thought, but memory was within my grasp for those few seconds, and now... Clare. Clare who? She wished she could picture what the woman looked like, but beyond that mass of dark hair she couldn't. She thought she was reasonably tall, maybe five foot seven or more - could she be a dancer? Or was she too tall for that? The frustration of the situation made her weep again.

In a way it was good that she had to think about the dancing classes again in the afternoon, and there was not time for too much soul searching. The children were a bit unruly, all very excited and wanting to tell her what they had for Christmas, and at the end of the session she felt she hadn't conducted a good class. Walking home she wondered if Julien had forgiven her for her outburst last night. I do love him, she thought, and I mustn't expect him to always sympathise with me over this memory business. I guess it's a bit of a pain to him quite often, yet he's usually so patient with me. She realised that he would be just as content for them to live together without the commitment of marriage; for herself she didn't know whether her need to know who she was in order to marry him stemmed from a puritanical streak in her or was the push she needed to unravel her past.

He came in with a bunch of spring flowers, just as she was cooking a meal.

'Julien, they're lovely. Daffodils in January - they must have cost the earth.'

He stayed for a meal of course, and although at first both studiously avoided mentioning the encounter at the theatre the previous evening, it had to come eventually.

'You were right,' she said, trying to be generous, 'it was so quick and there was nothing we could do, but oh you don't know how terrible it was to know I'd lost her.'

'I've been thinking about it a lot today too Daisy, and something occurred to me. She could well say to one of her friends, one of your mutual friends, "Guess who I saw last night. Clare... whatever your other name was. Haven't seen her for ages." And they could make an effort to track you down.'

'How?'

'By calling on wherever you used to live. Hang it all you must have lived somewhere. We don't know how well you knew her. You may have worked with her, known her casually. She didn't seem surprised to see you, did she? Just simply said, 'Hullo Clare,' as though she expected to run into you in such a place. I mean it wasn't a *whatever are you doing here* sort of thing, was it.'

Daisy laughed for the first time in twenty four hours. 'Oh Julien, you're absolutely right, but I may never bump into her again. It's as though she's tantalisingly given me one piece, one tiny piece of a huge jigsaw and I don't even know where that one piece fits in.'

Nevertheless, after that episode they went more often to the theatre, sometimes twice a week, and by the end of January they had seen almost everything on in London, but no-one again said, Hullo Clare. Not that she

126

expected it really, it was too farfetched to imagine that could happen twice.

One of her New Year Resolutions, one which she had kept defiantly to herself in case she found it too difficult to comply with, was to cease *actively* looking for her former self. To close the file as it were. She knew the niggle would always be with her, but the time had come to get on with her life. When you came up against a wall you couldn't walk through you had to divert and go round. With the theatre sighting that resolution went by the board. *Someone* in London knew her. As Julien had pointed out that person, whoever she was, knew other people, and among them possibly others who could give her back her identity. She dare not let the opportunity slip.

It was a strange feeling though, having finally decided *not* to pursue a will of the wisp, to be confronted with the first clue. Must be like the couples who long for a baby and when they stop thinking so hard about it, the miracle happens, she thought.

As the days passed it seemed to grow into more and more of a miracle, and it gave her a warm feeling. It's as though I've got proof now that I did *exist*, even if that proof is so flimsy.

Often she repeated the name *Clare* over and over to herself just before she went to sleep at night, in the hope that it would jog her dormant memory as she slumbered. And sometimes she woke in the morning repeating the name to herself, yet still it didn't yield the key she longed for - the one that would open the door to her former self, no matter what was behind it. Good or bad, at least then she would *know*.

Chapter 11

Jean and Phillip spent Christmas together. 'Sonia suggested it,' he said, almost sheepishly several weeks before. 'She has booked to go ski-ing with some friends and, well it's funny you know, but she's being so nice now. Helping all she can because of the baby. It's a side of her I have never seen before.'

Jean looked at him sharply, 'Perhaps she too has found someone else.'

'That's uncalled for. I believe it has something to do with her own childhood. She was illegitimate you see. She told me about it once and we have never spoken of it since. Yet I think it has motivated her whole life.'

Jean's voice softened. 'I'm sorry, Phillip. I just feel rather insecure, but I know I shouldn't, that it is going to be all right for us. That's why you knew she would agree to a divorce when you told her about the baby then?'

He nodded, 'I've always known that it went far deeper than she could ever tell me. Little things.' He shook himself visibly, as he brought his thoughts back to the matter in hand. 'Anyway it solves the Christmas holiday thing very well. We can be together and need have no guilty thoughts about Sonia. As long as she doesn't break a leg or something out there, which would complicate matters.' He squeezed her hand. 'That was meant to be a joke, darling.'

She didn't laugh although she smiled wanly at him. 'There is something else actually. Mummy and daddy have been in Spain for four years now and, I suppose it's because of Robert's death, but I had a letter the other day saying that they are coming back for Christmas and New Year.'

'There is only one thing you can do then. Tell them about us and the baby as quickly as possible.' He looked at her, 'It's going to be an awful shock otherwise.'

'I have drafted a letter, but I – well I wanted you to read it first. I've explained everything. Almost everything,' she corrected herself. 'I've told them that Robert and I were thinking about separating anyway, and that you and I are in love and are going to be married as soon as your divorce is through.'

'And the baby?'

'Yes, but I haven't said when. Just that I am pregnant.'

'What about your sister. Best to tie up all the loose ends now Jean, then we can settle properly when baby arrives.'

'She lives up north. I wrote to tell her about Robert and she telephoned and asked should she come down, but I put her off.'

'Best to write to her too I think. Now the thing is practically settled. Not that it would make any difference to either of us, would it?'

She did really smile then. Not a pale imitation. Was Phillip a tiny bit insecure too? Phillip who, like her, always had things cut and dried. Somewhere in his voice she detected an element of unsureness that she hadn't noticed before.

'What's funny?'

'Nothing really. It's just so nice to have someone who will think about these things and tie all the ends up. I have thought about it all but somehow, just lately I haven't seemed able to put any kind of plan into action.'

'You've had an awful lot on your plate darling, but from now on we share everything. Agreed?'

'Agreed Phillip. But it's still a shame about Christmas. It would have been a wonderful chance for us to be together. Just quietly together, instead of the stolen half hours when I can never remember all the things I want to say to you, and more and more I'm conscious of the rest of the world around us.'

'I know darling. Don't think I like this meeting in cafes for a quick lunch, with one eye on the clock and the other on the people who may be watching. I hate it as much as you do, but it will soon be over now. Then we can be together for always Jean.' He caught hold of her hand across the width of the table, his eyes devoured her with passion. 'I do love you Jean. I do want you so my darling.'

The following afternoon he telephoned. 'Jean, have you sent that letter to your parents yet?'

'No, I am going to do it in a minute and catch the evening post.'

'Well think about this idea. Let them come to you first, for a day and a night, and then go on to your sister because you and I are staying with friends over the Christmas. It won't be a lie because I have asked that hotel near Windsor to hold a booking for us. They're keeping it until tomorrow. What do you say?'

131

She wanted to say yes. To go away and be waited on appealed tremendously right now. Her usual energy had deserted her this last few weeks. Yet she hesitated.

'Phillip, darling, you're my choice and whatever they say or think will make no difference. But it would be nice not to quarrel with them. After all they are coming because of what happened, I'm sure of that.'

He surprised her by acquiescing without an argument. Whatever you think best darling. They are your parents. I'll tell the hotel not to hold the booking.'

A few days later she had a telephone call from Spain, 'You seem to have everything under control as usual,' her mother said, 'so how would it be if we came and met Phillip and left the following day. Then we could visit various friends on our way north, and possibly look in on you again briefly before returning. We shall be hiring a car of course, so travelling will be no problem. What do you think?'

She tried not to let the relief show in her voice. After all she wasn't a child, or even a young bride now, she was a mature woman who had in the past held a high level position at work. Her parents had liked Robert, they enjoyed his carefree attitude, his easy laughter, and they had known him for more than two years before they moved to Spain. Phillip was the unknown quantity for them.

'That sounds fine. And later, possibly, we may all be able to come out to visit you. When things have settled down,' she added, wondering why she was saying such things. Expecting a baby certainly changed a person's

132

normal temperament. Or was it Robert's death, and her knowledge of what had gone before that did it? Or even the strange situation she now found herself in. Previously she had been adamant that she never wanted to leave England, even for a holiday, but now...

Their meeting, although a bit strained, wasn't as emotional as Jean feared it might be. She felt more tearful when it was time for them to go than she would ever have expected. They did not speak a lot about Robert and she didn't tell them that he had in fact already left her on the day of the crash. She simply implied that he had been going to Torquay on business and they were going to talk about separation on his return.

'Our marriage wasn't working,' she said, 'but it was awful the way fate took a hand.' She liked that, it sounded right and proper, or as right and proper as it could under the circumstances. That was one of the things that bothered her, the fact that she could allow herself to be so unconventional. To be expecting another man's baby and even looking forward to it.

Although she would never have said it was the happiest Christmas of her life, she was able to be with the man she loved. The hotel they eventually booked now the arrangements had changed was only a few miles away. It wasn't one that gave lavish Christmas parties and she felt relieved about this. Of course Phillip would have checked, she thought, and not booked had that been the case. Her pregnancy was progressing well although she didn't always feel so good.

133

'The strain of what has happened,' Phillip said, 'no-one gets off scot free. I've even been having odd pains myself and I'm sure it's a mental reaction. I shall do as much as I can for Sonia, she won't be left destitute. When everything is settled we shall both feel much better because we are really conventional people, you and I.'

He looked so woebegone, sitting on the edge of the bed in his pyjamas, that she walked over and wound her arms round his neck. 'Of course we shall darling. We're two of a kind.'

She did appreciate not cooking the meal because she seemed to become very tired very quickly, and the smell of food cooking, although now well on in her pregnancy, still made her feel queasy.

Christmas was a pleasant interlude, but Jean longed now for it to be over and the divorce through so that she and Phillip could make the sort of plans she dare not think about until she was sure it would go through and he would be free to marry her.

'It's your legal mind, darling,' Phillip teased her, 'nothing is final until the contract is signed.'

She left work when she moved. Without saying so in words she implied that what her colleagues thought, that she was already pregnant when her husband died, was true.

Often she sat after her lunch, with a book on how to bring up baby, but her thoughts wandered from the printed words and she patted her stomach gently and wondered at how she had mellowed over these last few months. She had thought of herself as a career girl, children had not featured in her plans for many years. She knew people who had both, but that wasn't for her.

Her last pregnancy, when she lost the baby, was something she tried not to dwell on. Now she found herself watching people with a new attitude, and wondering what they were like as babies. Maybe that's why I didn't want to hurt mummy and daddy this time, she thought, because once I was probably their world as this baby inside me is mine now. It has to be, whether I want it that way or not because I am its only lifeline.

She wondered why she held out so long against Robert's freedom. Sometimes, during her rest periods in the afternoons, she thought about Robert's girlfriend. What was she like? Was she one of the dead in the train crash, or did she escape? If she did then she would have had to cope with the grief and not even be able to mourn publicly.

I didn't truly love Robert, it was probably infatuation in the beginning, or at the most a surface sort of love, and not the way I feel about Phillip. Maybe she, this unknown girl, and Robert had the depth of feeling, the kind of love that Phillip and I have. She discovered depths inside her she hadn't realised were there, like hoping the girl would find happiness again. Too late for Robert, but maybe not for her. In her mellow, motherhood mood she wanted the best for everyone; Robert's girl, even Phillip's wife, who, after all the stubborn months, was being so compassionate now.

They returned home for New Year and drank it in with champagne. Jean liked a glass of wine with a meal but, throughout her pregnancy, until now, had abstained. 'But after all, it is a special year for us, and one glass won't hurt,' she said. Raising their glasses to each other across an immaculately dressed dinner table, Phillip said, 'To the three of us and the future.'

He returned to work early in January and they married in February, two days after his divorce became absolute. Jean wore a pretty smock. She had scorned smocks at first and bought herself 'modern maternity wear', but nearing her time she found smocks the most comfortable form of dress. Phillip wore his best suit, a white shirt and dark red tie. Neither sported a buttonhole at Jean's request, 'We don't want the neighbours to realise we have only just been married.'

'You really do care what other people think, don't you, darling?'

'Don't you?' she countered.

'Yes, in as much as my career is concerned. I think I'd be all right but I would rather not take a chance. As far as anything else though, I don't give a damn. Still if it pleases you to keep them in ignorance, that's fine by me.'

Jean suspected that her attitude was a good let out for him too. He could pretend to be doing it all for her. The strange thing was that she didn't mind. She, who had said she would never pander to anyone was now taking that particular burden as her own.

After the ceremony they had a meal in a restaurant they had never been to before. 'So we shall have something to remember about our wedding apart from the vows we made darling,' Phillip said, surprising her yet again.

'Phillip, you really are a romantic at heart, aren't you? I never knew.'

'I'm as level headed as you, but, well,' he caught her hand across the table, 'you bring out the softness I me, Jean. I want you to look back to this day in five years' time, ten years' time, twenty, thirty, even forty and fifty years' time, and to remember it with love.'

Her eyes filled with tears. 'Phillip. Oh Phillip, my dear, my very dear.'

Her pains began that night when they were in bed, and in one of the lulls between them she said, 'My goodness, we were only just in time, weren't we?' which had her new husband laughing more than she had ever seen before.

Chapter 12

Janice, the girl in one of the flats from the large house next door was expecting a baby in February. She had many off days during the pregnancy when she felt too sick to do much.

'Really have to drag myself around,' she told Daisy one afternoon when they met in the street, 'but we need some shopping, so… someone told me the other day I'd have a good labour as I'm having a bad carrying time, so I hope they're right. Talk about an elephant, mine seems to have gone on for aeons. I can scarcely remember the last time I felt well – and flat,' she added with a wry smile.

'I'm out every day for my classes,' Daisy said, 'so if you don't feel like shopping I'll happily fetch anything you need.' After that encounter Daisy slipped next door most days to check before she went to her class.

Janice of course, knew nothing of her history, and Daisy had, over the months, become good at fending off personal questions.

'Are you an only child like me?' Janice asked her one day,' You've never mentioned any family.'

'Yes, I am. And no family either. I mean an orphan.'

'Gosh. I guess I'm pretty lucky really Daisy. Both my parents are still alive, although they live in Scotland and can't get down frequently. Of course with work we can't get up there more than once a year either. See my gran lives there and she needs looking after all the time, so they are pretty tied. Peter's going to take me up there when the babe's a few weeks old, and I'll stay for, probably a month. Unless I get too homesick,' she added with a grin.

Janice's baby arrived a few days earlier than expected and a glowing Peter told Daisy about his son before he went to work the following morning.

'He looks so tiny but he's a pair of lungs on him fit for an opera singer,' he said. 'I've been at the hospital all night and I'm just off to work now.'

The next day he came in again. 'You can go and see Janice if you'd like to,' he said, 'usually it's husbands and parents only at that hospital, but because Jan's folks aren't here Sister said one or two of her friends can go in.'

'I'll go after class, then the field will be clear for you in the evening,' she said, adding, 'I'm longing to see them both.'

She bought a tiny romper suit and a bib, wrapped them prettily, and when class finished that afternoon she set off for the maternity hospital.

Peter had told her there were three others in the ward. Two still waiting for their baby to arrive and one slightly older woman who had a son an hour after Janice. Daisy saw the Sister who directed her along the corridor to a side ward.

Janice was sitting on a chair by the bed nursing her baby, and as Daisy walked towards her she became aware of the other woman. Also in a chair with a baby in her arms, and she knew who it was.

In the few seconds that elapsed before she fainted she saw again, quite clearly, Robert, the only time he had shown her a photograph of his wife, Jean. In it she had

139

been holding her sister's baby, 'she is to be Godmother,' Robert said at the time. The pose now was exactly the same... Robert's wife, Robert, Robert, Ro...

She came round to find the Sister and a nurse with her. She struggled to sit up but they restrained her.

'Lie still a while longer, my dear. The doctor is on his way to have a look at you.'

'No, Sister, please. I'm all right, really I am. I don't need a doctor.'

'Nevertheless rest for another five minutes, then you can have a cup of tea.'

When she had gone the young nurse smiled at her, 'Feel better now? My but you startled the ladies in there.'

'How – how long was I – out, nurse?'

'Too long. That's why the doctor's coming to have a look at you. Are you pregnant dear?'

'No.' She didn't know what to think first, it was as though someone had pulled back the curtains and she was watching a play. Robert's wife – Robert's wife was in that ward with a baby, and she, Clare Disley, was going away with Robert. But it wasn't Robert's baby. It couldn't be because Robert was dead. She had extricated herself from his arms when the train crashed.

'I have to get out, please let me go home.' She was surprised to discover how weak she was as she tried to get off the bed. And even more surprised to find she was crying.

Sister returned with a doctor, who checked her over, asked her many questions, which she managed to parry. They mustn't know about the amnesia, the thought was

140

hammering away in her head. Now she knew who she was and what had happened to her she couldn't bear it if they delved.

Eventually they agreed that she could return home. 'Is there anyone who can come for you? There doesn't seem to be any physical reason why you fainted so suddenly and so deeply but you should take it easy for a few hours.'

'Julien. He'll come. What time is it please? Because I expect he will be home now.' Her mind seemed to be going frantic, but everything was there, the before and the after.

She drank a cup of too sweet tea, ate the biscuits they insisted on giving her, but was noticeably shaky when they suggested she could pop back into the ward and see Janice if she would like to. It was one thing to keep control of herself in this impartial recovery room, but how would she react to seeing Robert's wife again? The decision was taken out of her hands when Janice came in to see her.

'Sister said I could, and junior's gone to sleep. My but you gave us all a fright, Daisy. Are you OK?'

The past year of acting a role came to her rescue, although it seemed so strange to be addressed as Daisy now.

'I'm fine. And terribly sorry. Guess I've been rushing around a bit too much, and skipping lunch,' she added for good measure.

Julien was worried and it showed clearly in his expression. 'I've a taxi outside,' he said, 'can you walk?'

'Of course I can. Goodness I only fainted. Nothing to worry about.'

'They couldn't bring you round though. "A deep faint," the doctor called it. Come on, I'll take you home and tonight I'm doing the cooking while you put your feet up.'

She was silent during the ride back, but smiled in answer to Julien's anxious glances and leaned further against him. Once indoors she let the mask slip. 'Julien, I know why I fainted.'

His eyes searched her face tenderly and slowly she shook her head. 'No, I'm not pregnant. I remembered who I am and what I was doing on that train.'

It was his turn for shock. He sank onto the settee by her side. 'OK, I'm ready.'

Very quietly she began, 'My name is Clare Disley and I use to live with Auntie Margaret in Finchley. I'm a ballet dancer and I told her I was going abroad for two years with a new ballet company, but I wasn't. I was...' she paused to swallow some saliva, then looking straight at him she continued, 'I was starting a new life with Robert Jameson. He was married and his wife refused to divorce him. We were – we were going to Torquay to start together, we even gave ourselves a new name so we wouldn't be traced. Trebor, that's what we were going to be, Trebor – Robert the other way – R-R-Robert the other way round you see...' she couldn't go on as the pictures returned, the swaying train, she and Robert with a glass of wine in their hands, and the sudden wrench, blackness, then Robert's inert body.

142

Julien went out later to telephone Ian and Jill. 'I won't be long darling, but I'll go to a callbox because the one in the hall is a bit public, isn't it?'

'Tell them, please tell Ian I need to talk to him. Maybe I could go down for a few days – oh, there's the school.'

'We'll go at the weekend if Ian agrees. On Friday night.' He kissed her gently, 'leave it with me Daisy, and don't worry. Everything's going to be all right.'

Later that evening she thought about Auntie Margaret. 'Julien, we must go and see her. She'll be worried sick. You see I was going to contact her once – once we had settled in somewhere. Within a few weeks anyway. I was going to let her know where I was and who I was with. She – knew about Robert you see, and that we couldn't marry. Not a lot, but simply that there was this man. She's my only relative and I love her – I'd never leave her high and dry all this time.'

'Well it's Wednesday today and you aren't really in a fit state for that sort of reunion darling. How about tomorrow evening? Do you want to 'phone her first?'

'I don't know. Yes I think so – tell her – what can I tell her over the 'phone?'

'That you've been ill but are better now, and that you will explain everything when you see her in a few hours, or however long it will take us to get here. Where does she live?'

'Oh, in London Julien, in Finchley.' She looked relieved. 'You'll come, won't you?'

'I'll come, Daisy.'

'Do you, do you think you ought to call me Clare now? It seems strange to hear you say Daisy when I know I'm Clare. I – I suppose it's because I've always been Clare underneath.'

He put his arm round her. 'Daisy, Clare, it doesn't matter which, I love you, that's what matters. Remember I've only known you until now as Daisy, so I guess that's how I think of you, but I'll call you whatever you want me to sweetheart. All I'm asking is that you don't rush this thing, let it all happen gradually.'

'It isn't gradual, Julien. It's all there, like a film that's been stored. I'm not having to struggle to remember anything, it's just there as though someone pressed a switch. There's no strain and no jumble, everything I knew about me before I know now. My father was a parson and Auntie Margaret brought me up from the age of seven when he and my mother were killed on a church outing. They had accepted a lift in someone's car and the brakes failed.'

'A parson. That's why you felt so at home in churches I expect darling. Why you had that sense of peace and, yes and need too I think, when you were in a holy place.'

'I was very young when they died Julien, but Auntie Margaret, well she and I used to go to church together, and she always told me about them. Funny isn't it but I remember them too now. Shadowy memories of them, but always kept alive… oh Julien, how could I have forgotten Auntie Margaret? And, and…' she stopped, and he said gently, 'Robert?'

'Yes.'

'I don't understand any more than you do. I think we have to let it all sink in Daisy. Take things as they come, and the first of these is your aunt.'

Julien stood outside the telephone booth when she rang Auntie Margaret the following evening. 'She cried a little when she heard my voice Julien. Poor darling, she must have been worried. She said she tried to find me when there were no letters or cards, and no-one seemed to know or even have heard of the company. Julien I feel awful. I never expected anything like that to happen. I planned to be in touch with her within weeks...' she rubbed her eyes viciously.

'You'll be there in twenty minutes darling, so dry your eyes and smile. Let her see you happy, eh?'

Jill telephoned her the following day. 'Are you all right Daisy?'

'I think so Jill.'

'Ian has been to the police and told them that your memory has returned and that you were travelling with a Mr Robert Jameson. They said a man was identified as Robert – are you still there Daisy?'

'Yes, yes. Go on please.'

'He had no documents on him but his wife and a great friend who knew him well identified him beyond reasonable doubt.'

'So Robert's wife eventually found him, Julien,' she said when she returned upstairs. 'Poor woman. It must have been as much a shock for her as it was for me to see her in that hospital. I mean he had left her some money and a note saying he wasn't coming back. But – not for

145

that reason.' She bowed her head as though she was saying a prayer. In her heart she was.

'The police, the police must have contacted her, though how I don't know because, like me, he had no means of identification on him.'

'Probably we shall never know how.'

'When I spoke to the police just after Christmas they said everyone had been identified. To think everyone included Robert – and I couldn't even remember him.' Her eyes filled with tears and Julien said gently, 'Do you want to talk about it, or would you rather wait for Ian?'

'I don't know. In a way it's as though it's only just happened. I mean, I know it hasn't, and – and Robert's been dead almost a year now, but, but for me it's only just happened. How you could wipe something like that so completely from your mind seems appalling.'

'Because it was so appalling for you that your mind shut it out'.

'But usually, according to Ian and the doctor at the hospital, only for a short time, hours maybe. Not months and months and months. I'm so confused Julien, so utterly confused...'

'Darling, darling Daisy – Clare – somehow we'll work through it together. The great thing is not to rush it, I'm sure.'

They went to Torquay for the weekend, but first they paid another visit to Aunt Margaret. She was so relieved that Clare had come back to her. 'I thought you must be dead; I even went to the Italian Embassy to try to check out ballet companies operating there. I knew you

146

wouldn't not get in touch if you could and you hear such dreadful things…'

There was so much catching up to do yet Clare had no heart for it. As the hours went by she found herself thinking more and more about Robert, and that night in bed the tears came. All the love she had for him, all the dreams they had to fulfil together and now… once, in the early hours of the morning she relived the terrible moment when she crawled out from beneath his body and knew he was dead. That was the cut-off point – that was where memory had stopped.

The amazing thing was that she hadn't been injured. Robert's body had protected her, saved her life probably… thumping the pillow in her anguish she cried desperately for her lost love.

Somehow she carried on with her normal activities. In a way it was a blessing that she had the school and had to go and teach. For that period anyway she wasn't thinking about Robert. She didn't think much about Julien either during that first forty eight hours of memory return, and when, just as they were leaving her aunt's house, Margaret said to him, 'Come round anytime with Clare. I hope I'll be seeing you again,' he replied, almost wistfully, 'I hope so too.'

The sadness in his voice brought it home to her suddenly and very forcefully. Julien. She had committed herself to Julien and now she was sorrowing for Robert. She felt nearly as mixed up now as she had when she didn't know who she was. Then she didn't seem to have been anybody, now she was two people, Robert's Clare, and Julien's Daisy.

They drove to Torquay on the Saturday morning because Clare was too exhausted Friday evening. Whenever she had thought about the return of her memory, which was frequently, she saw it as a wonderful happening. Wariness for the mystery of why she was travelling incognito but offset by joy to know the details of her own life once more. But it wasn't a bit like that. Her overwhelming grief that Robert was dead cast a shadow over everything else. That first euphoria was lost in the incredible heartache she felt.

Very conscious now of Julien by her side she felt guilty about loving him. How could she have forgotten Robert? She twisted the ring on her finger and fought off memories of the night he had placed it there.

Julien had been so patient. He said once, 'So you aren't married, darling, and later the way will be clear for us.' She saw his startled and disappointed look when she hadn't answered, but he had not followed up his remark, and for this she was grateful.

Jill hugged her without words and Ian kissed her and murmured softly, 'You talk about it in your own time. We've the entire weekend free.'

Sarah was out, 'but she'll be back later and she's longing to see you. She wanted to wait until you arrived, but the arrangements were already made.'

It was like coming home. Almost as much as it had been returning to Aunt Margaret's. Within minutes there was tea and sandwiches, 'just to fortify you now,' Jill said, 'I've a nice piece of beef for tonight.'

She didn't know where to begin, how to tell these dear friends that she had been 'eloping' with a married man. Put like that it sounded so terrible, yet at the time... and there was Julien. Julien whom she loved, or thought she did – had been sure of it until her memory returned. How could she so quickly have discarded the old for the new, even if she did not then remember the old. Surely something of it would have stayed, buried beneath that dark curtain that had hung down for so long.

It was Ian who suggested that if Julien wanted to visit his parents now might be a good time. 'We'll look after Daisy, you know that, don't you? And then we can all settle down for the evening.'

Julien looked at her, and she said, 'Yes, do that Julien. I'll be fine and – and you've heard the story several times already. Give them – give them – my fond wishes, and ask them to forgive me not coming this time. Later, later, I will.'

'They'll understand. Sure you don't mind? I ought to pop in – well I want to pop in,' he corrected himself. 'I won't be very late.'

When he had gone Jill said, 'Julien told us on the 'phone about Robert, and – and about what happened. Do you want us to call you Clare now?'

'I don't know. Parts of being Daisy have been so good, better than some parts of being Clare. That confused Julien too when I asked him to call me Clare. I am worried,

149

now he's not here I can say, but did I fall in love with him because I needed someone, or because it was real?'

Jill looked at her husband. 'Over to you Ian. You're the doctor.'

He lit his pipe and gazed at her, 'Jill's always had a neat way of passing the buck Daisy. But deep down you know the answer to that. And you have got so into the habit of asking yourself questions, and trying to find motives that you aren't likely to accept much at face value for a while. I think you fell in love with him – full stop. Most of us are capable of loving more than one person during our lifetime you know.'

Jill pulled a face but kept silent, and Clare murmured softly, 'Go on.'

'Your life took a different turning after the accident. It would have done so anyway, but the amnesia was an added burden. If you had retained your memory, who's to say you wouldn't still have stayed in Torquay, met Julien and fallen in love with him? What you are experiencing now is something we talked about before – grief. You will need a period of mourning. Some of the healing may have taken place already, but most of it is still to be done I think.'

'Do you – do you think very badly of me going off with a married man?'

It was Jill who answered. 'Daisy, look at me – look at us please. Don't lower your head like that. We accepted you as a friend when we knew nothing and neither of us will change now you have a background. It's you we care about, the inside you.'

'I feel so guilty. I think I've had this feeling of guilt all through really, even though I couldn't remember what it was for. It was the only thing that marred our happiness, Robert's and mine, and I thought I should be able to beat it in the end, but, but, it wasn't meant. I didn't get a chance to see...' Jill held out her arms.

Clare began to relax. Down here with these people who knew her story, these people she had learned to love, she was safe. For so long now she felt threatened when talk turned to personal affairs – now she was no longer in the dark and she could choose how much or how little to tell people. The important thing was that she knew. She knew about her own life. It had never seemed that important before.

They talked until the room was in shadow, and the gentle light from the undrawn curtains shone onto their faces, illuminating them like flickering lamps. She found she could tell them about Robert, about the ceremony of placing the ring on her finger, about the laughter that bubbled out of him over so much, and about that gentle, serious Robert who always surfaced for a brief spell with her, even in the midst of fun. A look, a touch, an endearment...

She was surprised to discover the tears on her cheeks when Jill finally switched on the lights and drew the curtains.

'Oh my goodness,' she said, endeavouring to rub them away, 'but I do feel better.'

When Sarah came in, and later when Julien returned, she was almost in charge of her emotions again. And

151

Sarah's exuberant and over-the-top greetings made her smile rather than cry which was a relief.

Before leaving Torquay on Sunday, they visited Maudie. 'A flying visit,' Clare said, 'but I wanted you to know the news that my memory has returned.' After the first few moments Maudie did not probe. 'I'm dying to hear everything, but in your own time my dear. I can see you aren't ready yet.'

Julien was exceptionally quiet on the return journey. She was too at first – it had been an emotionally if not physically exhausting weekend. When they stopped for a drink halfway back they found a table for two in a corner of the restaurant, and he said very quietly, 'You all right?'

'Mmm. I'm glad we went. It's cleared a lot of things up in my mind, Julien.'

'I'm not sure if I should be happy or sad about that. Now you have your life back – your other life I mean, you may not want the new one.'

His eyes smiled at her, but there was no merriment in them, more of a wistful sadness.

'What makes you say that?'

'I don't think I've existed for you since you knew. Not in the way I did before. You know I'm here but you're not really seeing me any more are you Daisy?'

She leaned across the small table. 'Yes I am Julien. Please bear with me. I have to adjust to all my remembering. And my guilt.'

'Guilt?'

'Yes. But I will, and that's a promise from – from both of us, Clare and Daisy.'

He stroked her fingers gently. 'I'll try my darling, I'll try.'

They drank their tea and returned to the carpark.

'Julien, I do love you,' she said as he opened the car door for her. 'That won't change. Not my feelings. Not now. But my pretence at being a widow wasn't so far wrong really. Only I couldn't remember who I was mourning. Now I do know I need time. I'm so lucky to have found two people in my lifetime whom I've loved and who have loved me. If you still want me later, not too much later.. my dear...'

They were standing very close together now. 'As much time as you need sweetheart. I'll be here for you, forever.'

They fell into each other's arms, to the delight of an elderly couple who pulled in and parked next to them.

'Takes you back, doesn't it?' the silver haired woman said, 'Oh to be young as those two again.'

He squeezed her hand, 'But we have something very precious that they haven't had time to find yet.'

Her eyes smiled into his. 'What's that?'

'Memories, my dear, precious memories.'

THE END

www.ingramcontent.com/pod-product-compliance
Lightning Source LLC
Chambersburg PA
CBHW020134180626
46810CB00004B/1544